Five Nights at Freddy's
TALES FROM THE PIZZAPLEX

#8 B7-2

Five Nights at Freddy's
TALES FROM THE PIZZAPLEX

#8 B7-2

BY

**SCOTT CAWTHON
KELLY PARRA
ANDREA WAGGENER**

Scholastic Inc.

If you purchased this book without a cover, you should be aware that this book is stolen property. It was reported as "unsold and destroyed" to the publisher, and neither the author nor the publisher has received any payment for this "stripped book."

Copyright © 2023 by Scott Cawthon. All rights reserved.

Photo of TV static: © Klikk/Dreamstime

All rights reserved. Published by Scholastic Inc., *Publishers since 1920*. SCHOLASTIC and associated logos are trademarks and/or registered trademarks of Scholastic Inc.

The publisher does not have any control over and does not assume any responsibility for author or third-party websites or their content.

No part of this publication may be reproduced, stored in a retrieval system, or transmitted in any form or by any means, electronic, mechanical, photocopying, recording, or otherwise, without written permission of the publisher. For information regarding permission, write to Scholastic Inc., Attention: Permissions Department, 557 Broadway, New York, NY 10012.

This book is a work of fiction. Names, characters, places, and incidents are either the product of the author's imagination or are used fictitiously, and any resemblance to actual persons, living or dead, business establishments, events, or locales is entirely coincidental.

Library of Congress Cataloging-in-Publication Data available

ISBN 978-1-338-87397-9

10 9 8 7 6 5 4 3 2 1   23 24 25 26 27

Printed in the U.S.A.   131

First printing 2023 • Book design by Jeff Shake

TABLE OF CONTENTS

B7-2 _____ 1

Alone Together _____ 73

Dittophobia _____ 137

B7-2

THE VOICES WERE FAR AWAY BUT GETTING CLOSER. THEY WERE LIKE SCRATCHY STATIC MARRING THE CLARITY OF A PERFECT MELODY. UNTIL THE VOICES HAD INTRUDED, BILLY HAD BEEN FLOATING IN A SWEET HAZE OF SENSATION-FREE BLISS. NOW THE VOICES CUT THROUGH THAT BLISS, YANKING BILLY INTO A MUDDLE OF NOISE AND PAIN.

Billy threw up a hand, wanting to ward off the invading unpleasant feelings. His raised hand, though, brought even more pain—a sharp, cutting sting. Billy gasped and opened his eyes.

The pinpoint lights were blinding. He snapped his eyes shut again. The bliss was well and truly gone now.

Billy's senses flooded with information. Even through his closed lids, he could see the spears of bright light. He could hear loud chatter and a few shouts combined with an insistent and grating beep, the patter of footsteps, and the occasional metallic clatter. He smelled the pungent scents of bleach and disinfectant, the acrid odor of urine, and the nauseating smell of overcooked vegetables—maybe broccoli and cabbage. He felt something pricking at the back of his right hand, but that was the least of the pain he felt. It seemed like nearly every nerve ending in his body was firing a barrage of throbs and aches and twinges. Everything hurt. And the taste in his mouth . . . Billy tried to move his tongue around to erase the bitterness that was so powerful, and he had to swallow down a gag. But then he remembered that he had very little tongue remaining. Only the barest nubbin of tissue was able to wiggle around in his mouth, and it could do nothing to wipe away the caustic flavor.

Billy opened his eyes again. Turning his head away from the lights, he blinked several times and looked around. He was definitely in the hospital. But why?

Frowning, Billy dug through his distorted memories. He saw himself looking in the mirror, gazing at his unnaturally square face and his mutilated body. He saw the floor of his home, and he remembered lying on it, crying. He saw his neighborhood, and he remembered lurching through it, walking and walking. He saw a junkyard and an old station wagon, and he felt himself climbing into the back of it.

TALES FROM THE PIZZAPLEX

The compactor, Billy thought. The last thing he remembered was the feeling of compression, a system-wide pain that blotted out all his sadness and regret.

The memory acted like a catalyst, and now his mind replayed his recalled experience of listening to the rumble of the big machine that bore down on the car he'd hidden in. That sound, for some reason, pulled him back into his identity. He instantly became aware of it all; he simultaneously integrated the personality of a boy whose play had turned into a yearslong delusion and of a man who had realized his horrible mistakes and had to face his remorse and self-hate.

That compactor had been Billy's way out of all of it—his surrender. So how did he . . . ?

"Well, look who has joined us!" a perky voice cried out.

Billy turned his head toward the open doorway. A compact woman with short, strawberry blonde curls and a heavily freckled oval face bustled up to the side of the bed Billy lay in. The woman wore a bright blue cotton uniform; maybe she was a nurse. Glancing at the beeping monitors, she put warm, smooth fingers against the back of Billy's right hand. And he could feel them.

Why could he feel the nurse's fingers?

As quickly as Billy had cycled through the mind pictures that reminded him of the last thing he remembered before being in this room, Billy's brain flooded him with an awareness of his life. Instantly, Billy knew that he had prosthetic limbs—he *knew* he did. And although the limbs often seemed real to him, he wasn't able to feel anything with them.

Billy lifted his head so he could get a better view of his right arm. He groaned involuntarily when sudden dizziness and a knifelike pain made it clear that his head protested the sudden movement.

"Careful there," the nurse said. "You've been through a lot, and you've been unconscious a long time. You're going to feel discomfort and disorientation."

Billy looked around, hoping to see the computer he'd used to communicate with after he'd had his tongue removed. There was no computer. He'd have to try to talk.

He opened his mouth. But the words he wanted to say wouldn't come out.

"Here," the nurse said. "Your mouth has to be super dry." She reached over to a nightstand that Billy hadn't noticed when he'd looked around.

Billy focused on the gray metal stand now, and he saw it held a mustard-yellow plastic pitcher and a couple of small paper cups. One of the cups held water and a little sponge on a stick. The nurse moved the sponge, pulled a straw from her pocket, and put the straw in the cup. She held the straw to Billy's mouth.

"Go slow," she warned.

Billy tentatively raised his head. This time, the room didn't spin as much, and the pain wasn't as intense. He used his lips to suck water through the straw. As he did, he glanced at the white name tag pinned to the nurse's uniform. Her name was Gloria.

When Gloria pulled the straw away from Billy and set the cup back on the nightstand, he said, "Thank you, Gloria."

Or at least that's what he tried to say. What came out was actually more like "Ank oo, Oria." And the *K* was off. It wasn't crisp and clear—it sounded like something stuck in Billy's throat.

"Not bad!" Gloria said brightly. "Without a full tongue, you're going to have trouble with a lot of the letters. But don't worry—we'll get you set up with a speech therapist. That will help you out."

Billy nodded, but he didn't care about that. He had so many questions he wanted answered now.

"How?" he asked. What he really wanted to get out was *How did I survive being crushed in the car?* But that was too many words.

"I'm going to call for Dr. Herrera," Gloria said. "She's been in charge of your surgeries and has overseen your recovery. She'll explain everything. You'll like her. She's super nice." Gloria leaned over and checked the line that was connected to the back of Billy's right hand. "Looking good," she said. "But if the line starts to bug you, or you need anything else, just press this." She pointed at a button on a small remote control that dangled from a thick white cord over the railing on the right side of Billy's bed. Billy stretched out his fingers to make sure he could reach the button. He was in awe that his fingers were still there.

Gloria walked around the bed and adjusted his covers. Then she patted his left leg.

Billy widened his eyes in surprise. He could feel that, too. How was that possible?

"Just hang tight," Gloria said. "Dr. Herrera will be in here in a jiff."

A "jiff" turned out to be about a half hour. Billy was able to note the time because he could see a big black-numbered clock on the wall above the nursing station outside his room. It was 1:42 (p.m., obviously, because the sun was out) when Gloria left the room, and it was 2:14 when Dr. Herrera walked in.

Even wearing a baggy white lab coat over the same blue cotton uniform that Gloria wore, Dr. Herrera looked more like a Hollywood star than a doctor. Dark skinned and black haired, the thirtysomething, tall, slender woman had large, deep-set, heavily lashed brown eyes; sculpted cheekbones; a strong jaw; and a full mouth with even, white teeth. Obviously adept with makeup, Dr. Herrera had accented all her naturally beautiful features perfectly. Billy thought that her smoky eye shadow and red lipstick made her look like she was ready for a photo shoot. He had never met a woman as stunning as Dr. Herrera; he'd only seen women like her in pictures or on TV.

"Billy," Dr. Herrera said with a smile as she approached his bed, "it's wonderful to see you awake and alert."

Dr. Herrera's deep, even voice was as warm as her eyes were. Billy, however, found himself tensing when she stepped up next to the bed, pulled a stethoscope from her pocket, and put it to her ears. When she bent over him and pulled down the neck of the baby-blue thin cotton hospital gown he wore, he held his breath. He suddenly was aware that the gown only covered the front of him. He felt exposed and vulnerable, and he flinched as Dr. Herrera placed the hard, cold end of the stethoscope against his bare chest.

In spite of the way Dr. Herrera seemed—nice—her white coat and stethoscope and her title—*doctor*—immediately brought up memories of Doc, the grizzled old guy who'd turned Billy into the monster he'd discovered himself to be hours before he'd made his way to the junkyard. Billy knew that Doc had only done what Billy had asked him to do, but that didn't mitigate Billy's association of Doc with all the pain he'd gone through. Billy hated the idea of another doctor looming over him. He didn't want to be in a doctor's control.

"Your heart sounds good," Dr. Herrera said, straightening.

Billy exhaled in relief when Dr. Herrera stepped away from his bed and pulled out the brown vinyl chair, which was straight-backed and didn't look comfortable, toward the foot of the bed. She placed the chair where Billy could easily see her without craning his neck, and she took a seat.

"Okay," Dr. Herrera said. "Let's get you caught up on what's been going on. Sound good?"

Still feeling intimidated and wary, Billy managed a nod. He needed to know what had happened, so he forced himself to stay calm and listen.

Dr. Herrera clasped her large hands together.

"Okay," Dr. Herrera said again. She said the word with a long O sound: oookay.

Dr. Herrera opened her mouth and then closed it. "Perhaps we should start with what you remember," she said.

In spite of his nervousness, Billy found himself relaxing a little. Dr. Herrera spoke with a slight accent—Billy thought it was maybe Spanish—and the ebb and flow of her words were strangely soothing.

Billy cleared his throat. "I remember going to the junkyard and getting in the old car, and I remember the car was being crushed."

These words were what Billy heard in his mind when he spoke, but what he heard in his ears was much different. Without a tongue, Billy could only clearly use a few letters—*A, B, E, F, I, M, O, P, R, V,* and *Y*—without distortion. Some letters—*K, Q, U,* and *X*—were close but somewhat garbled. The rest of the letters—those that required pressing his tongue to the roof of his mouth in any way—weren't accessible at all. Consequently, his speech was mushy and difficult to understand. Somehow, though, Dr. Herrera managed to grasp the gist of what Billy had said.

"That's what I thought," Dr. Herrera said. "After you were found, the police at first thought you'd been attacked and placed in the vehicle compactor against your will. They had to go to your home and investigate. When they did that, they found out the truth."

Billy pressed his lips together. He hated the idea of strangers going through his things. He could feel his heart rate speeding up. He forced himself to breathe slowly. At least he didn't have to explain anymore.

"Why am I alive?" Billy asked.

"Well, to start with," Dr. Herrera said. "Dumb luck apparently. No one is sure why you survived the machine, but you did. And you were found just in time because the junkyard owner is a bird-watcher. He said he spotted a rare bird on the hood of the station wagon. That's when he noticed blood coming out from under the wagon's back door. It was almost too late. You suffered severe injuries. You had a cracked skull, jaw, collarbone, and pelvis, and your right arm and left leg were fractured. You also had internal injuries—some damage to your liver, kidneys, spleen, and gallbladder. Plus, you had a collapsed lung when they brought you in. In addition to that, you had all the modifications you underwent before the compactor injuries. We dealt with your injuries and we removed all the foreign materials and parts from your body in a series of surgeries. During that time and for several weeks after, we've kept you in a medically induced coma to give your body the time it needed to heal." Dr. Herrera studied Billy's face. "And your body has done a fine job, I have to say."

Considering how much Billy hurt, he wasn't sure about that. But he didn't say anything. He was struggling to comprehend the fact that all the additions he'd made to his body had been removed. So why was so much of him still here? His memory told him that he'd been nearly entirely replaced with metal and wire and plastic.

Glancing down at his clearly intact right hand, Billy had to question his take on what he'd done to himself. Obviously, he had it wrong. But why?

Dr. Herrera shifted in the brown chair. Billy refocused on her.

"Some of the work you had done couldn't be undone," Dr. Herrera said. "Your right leg and left arm were amputated. The exterior cartilage of your ears has been removed, and most of your tongue is missing. The rest of your body, however, was integrated with the foreign material. Oddly, your left leg had been surgically altered to appear as if it had been amputated, and prosthetic materials had been incorporated with your flesh. According to the files the police found in your house, you asked the doctor to remove all your limbs, but it appears he got lazy, or maybe greedy—he took your money and didn't do one of the amputations. He just made modifications so it appeared that the amputation was done." Dr. Herrera shook her head then went on, "The police raided the old mental hospital where your doctor did his surgeries, and they found body parts in a freezer. Not all were yours, but some were... including your right arm. We're able to reattach parts when they're preserved well enough."

Billy looked down at his right arm in awe. Dr. Herrera smiled and crossed her legs.

"As for the rest," Dr. Herrera said, "when I removed all of what shouldn't have been there, it came out as one coherent piece, all the extraneous parts held together with wires and your own connective tissue and flesh."

Billy winced at the idea of what must have gone into removing that from his body and at the idea of losing even more of himself in the process. His stomach clenched.

Dr. Herrera leaned forward and touched Billy's right hand. Billy thought she meant the gesture as one of comfort, but it just made his stomach flip over again. He wanted to yank his hand away from her, but he was too scared. The idea of this woman slicing him open and taking out what had essentially been a cobbled-together animatronic endoskeleton brought up memories of the time Billy had spent in Doc's basement. Billy couldn't contain a shiver, but Dr. Herrera didn't seem to notice it.

"The work that was done on you," Dr. Herrera went on, "although unconscionable and gruesome, was unlike anything I've seen. Because of that, I had put what we removed in one of our storage vaults downstairs." Dr. Herrera cocked her head. "Do you have any questions, Billy?"

Billy had a lot of questions, but he didn't want to ask any of them. Still marveling at his intact right arm, he finally managed to lift it. Trailing the line that was inserted into the back of his hand, he brought his fingers to his face. Not sure what he'd feel, he tentatively touched his cheek.

"Would you like a mirror?" Dr. Herrera asked.

Billy hesitated, then nodded.

"I thought you might," Dr. Herrera said.

She reached into the pocket of her white coat and pulled out a hand mirror. Standing, Dr. Herrera stepped toward the head of Billy's bed and held the mirror out in front of him. Billy took a deep breath and looked at his reflection.

The last time Billy had inspected himself, what he'd seen was nothing like what he was seeing now. Gone were the hard edges created by the metal plating. Gone were the black eyes. Gone was the bare skull.

Yes, Billy's ears were still missing, but other than that, he looked pretty normal. He even saw a bit of his dad in the small eyes and nose, round cheeks, and wide mouth that he saw in the mirror.

As it had when Billy was a child, Billy's brown hair was sticking up haphazardly in a variety of directions. His hair was maybe three inches long—obviously, he'd been in the coma for quite some time.

If the hair itself hadn't been a hint of the passed time, the condition of Billy's scars told the rest of the story. When Billy had imagined Dr. Herrera cutting into him and taking out all the extra parts, he'd envisioned jagged incisions crusted with blood and tied with stark black thread. Instead, what he saw were faintly red scars bracketing his cheeks, forehead, and jaw. Clearly, he was well on his way to healing from his wounds.

Billy tried to take the mirror from Dr. Herrera's hand, but he found that his fingers wouldn't work quite right. Dr. Herrera shifted the mirror as she gestured with her other hand at Billy's right arm.

"You're going to be a little stiff after being out for so

long," she said. "You got passive physical therapy while you were out—manual movement of your limbs to keep the muscles limber and prevent too much loss of muscle mass. However, you'll need physical therapy so you can learn to use a crutch with the right arm until your right leg is ready for a new prosthetic."

Billy shook his head violently. "No!" he shouted. The word came out as a long and loud "Oh." Billy locked his gaze on Dr. Herrera. "No more prosthetics!" The words sounded like "O or rohehik."

Dr. Herrera seemed to get it. She pulled the mirror away from him and stuck it back in her pocket as she soothed, "It's okay, Billy. We won't do anything you don't want." She gently put a hand on Billy's shoulder. In spite of his fear of her, the touch felt good.

Dr. Herrera backed up and sat down again. "Obviously," she said, "we had to do everything we did without your consent because you weren't able to give it." She leaned toward Billy. "Some of my colleagues didn't think we'd be able to save you, but I knew we could. And we have . . . with a lot of help from you." She gestured at Billy's prone form. "Your body's ability to heal has been quite extraordinary. You've come much further much faster than anyone could have predicted, and I expect you'll get your strength back in no time. Our part is pretty much done. From here on out, with some exceptions, choices about what's done to continue your healing will be up to you."

Billy scrunched up his forehead. Exceptions? He opened his mouth to try to form the word.

Dr. Herrera held up a hand. "I know what you're thinking. 'What exceptions?' Right?"

Billy nodded.

13

Dr. Herrera nodded, too. She took a long breath and exhaled. "I don't want to overload you with too much right now," she said. "You're still healing. But you might as well know that social services assigned you an advocate. Because of what the police found in your house, the state is requiring a psychological evaluation now that you're out of your coma. That's nonnegotiable. But if you're deemed competent, you'll get to call the shots going forward."

You'll get to call the shots. Dr. Herrera's words echoed in Billy's head long after she left his room.

What would that be like now? Billy wondered. Would he be able to make good decisions about his life?

The last thing Billy remembered before succumbing to the pain of the compactor had been a crushing feeling of loss. That was why letting the compactor press down on him had felt so right, so welcome.

Now Billy was being given a second chance. He could make a whole new set of decisions. He could have a new life—the life he'd thought he'd missed out on forever.

That thought was both exciting and terrifying. Given that Billy couldn't remember choosing anything for himself that wasn't part of his animatronic delusion, he didn't know how he'd decide what to do next.

But he didn't have to face that right away. He would be in the hospital for a while longer. For that, Billy was grateful.

In just the short time Billy had been conscious in his barren hospital room, it had started to feel like a welcome haven. He liked its plain walls and its louvered blinds, which he asked Gloria to lower after Dr. Herrera left. Billy liked the little room, but the big blue sky outside felt threatening for some reason. All that sunshiny openness was too much for him to process.

A couple hours after Dr. Herrera left him, Billy got to eat his first meal as his new self. Having spent most of his life eating the "animatronic diet" of only white foods, he was eager to try something new. Unfortunately, the evening meal was chicken and rice with green beans. The chicken and rice were familiar, and therefore unwelcome. But he eagerly dug into the green beans. They didn't taste as good as he'd hoped they would, but the red Jell-O dessert was wonderful. In his new life, Billy decided, he'd eat a lot of red foods.

The second day of Billy's new life, he met his physical therapist, Angie. On one side of Angie's head, her hair was shorn into a buzz cut; on the other side, her hair was long and woven into a complicated braid. Angie didn't look like she was very strong, but Billy quickly found out that she was.

Angie came into Billy's room carrying an armful of bandages, a leg brace, and a crutch. "Okay, Billy," she said after she'd introduced herself. "We need to get you up on your feet. Or foot, as the case may be." She grinned at him.

Billy laughed, but his muscles were tense. Did he really want to try to stand up?

Billy's memory of being on his feet wasn't a good one. He clearly remembered the way he'd careened down the sidewalk to the junkyard where he'd thought he was going to die. And that had been with both prosthetics. Now he had one leg still recovering from surgery, and the other leg was completely gone. How would he stand?

"I hear you," Angie said.

"I didn't say anything," Billy said.

"You didn't have to. Your trepidation is written all over your face."

"*Trepidation* is a good word," Billy said.

"Glad you like it." Angie lowered the railing on the left side of Billy's bed.

Earlier that morning, Gloria had removed all the lines that had connected Billy to the monitors that had clustered around his bed. "Your vital signs are perfect," Gloria had said. "Dr. Herrera says you don't need monitoring anymore."

Gloria had then looked at Billy's IV. "How's your pain?" she had asked.

Billy thought about it. He was surprised to realize that the aches and throbs he'd felt when he'd first woken up had abated a lot. He was sore, but he wasn't in agony. "Not bad," he said.

"Good," Gloria said. "You haven't had any meds going through this line since last night. Just glucose. And now you're eating on your own. So, let's get this thing out of you." She proceeded to remove the IV that had been poking into the back of his right hand. Billy was happy to get rid of that.

Now that he was no longer plugged into anything, Billy could move more freely. Even so, he was wary when Angie leaned over him and said, "Go ahead and put your arm around my neck."

The idea of doing this made Billy very uncomfortable. He felt hesitant and self-conscious.

"Come on," Angie said. "Don't be shy. I'm tough." She grinned at him.

Billy smiled. He did as she told him to do.

Over the next hour, Angie got Billy sitting up and

then, after bandaging his remaining leg and encasing it in a black, padded brace, she taught him how to use a crutch with his remaining arm. Between the crutch and braced leg, Billy managed to not only stand but also walk out of his room and down the hall.

"You're amazing!" Angie said at the end of the hour. "Dr. Herrera said you healed unusually fast. She was right."

Angie helped Billy get back into bed, which was harder than he'd thought it would be. *Maybe he'd overdone it,* he thought. Some of the pain he'd felt the day before was returning.

"You're probably going to be sore," Angie said. "Using a crutch is no picnic. When you get new prosthetics, moving around will be a lot easier."

Billy immediately felt the same horror he'd felt when Dr. Herrera had mentioned new prosthetics. He vehemently shook his head. "I don't want new prosthetics," he told Angie.

Angie crossed her arms over her hot-pink cotton uniform top. "Whyever not? They'll give you a much better life."

Billy kept shaking his head. He was surprised when his eyes even filled with tears.

Angie perched on the edge of Billy's bed. She put her hand lightly on his chest. "It's okay," she said softly. Her voice was much gentler than it had been when she'd been barking orders at him while she helped him learn to use the crutch. "I get it," Angie said. "I heard what happened to you. You went through hell. And if I was you, I'd feel the same way about adding something else to my body. But, Billy," Angie's voice softened even more, "before, you were using the prosthetics to try to be something you weren't. If you get them now, you'll be using them to become yourself again."

Billy pursed his lips. He understood what Angie was saying, but the idea of doing anything else to his body was terrifying.

"You don't have to take any action now, obviously," Angie said. "But if I were you, I would keep the option open. Revisit the idea when you feel better."

Billy nodded. He was too rattled to speak.

Angie pushed off the bed and gave him a thumbs-up. "I'll be back in the morning for another torture session." She winked at him.

That made Billy laugh. He decided he'd do what she suggested. Maybe sometime in the future, he'd rethink the prosthetics.

The third day of Billy's new life started with another walking session with Angie. In addition to helping him get more comfortable using the crutch, Angie showed him how to raise and lower the rails on his bed, and she had him practice—three times—getting himself from the bed to the bathroom so he could use the toilet. Billy was surprised and pleased when he was able to manage that task.

Not long after Angie left him, Billy had the psychological evaluation Dr. Herrera had told him about. This was done by a grim-faced bald man named Dr. Coleman, someone Billy didn't like at all. *Dr. Coleman*, Billy thought, *didn't like Billy, either.* Dr. Coleman's questions were curt, and Dr. Coleman kept staring at Billy's ears— or rather, where Billy's ears should have been. Billy was glad when Dr. Coleman left.

After Dr. Coleman was gone, Gloria came in to check on Billy. When she found him touching what remained of his ears, she looked into his eyes. "Are you okay?"

"Dr. Coleman was disgusted by my ears," Billy said. "I could tell."

Gloria rolled her eyes. "Don't get me started on Dr. Coleman."

"But he's right," Billy said. "My ears are ugly."

"Not ugly," Gloria said. "Just different."

"I need a hat," Billy said.

Gloria shook her head. Billy crossed his arms and nodded. Gloria shrugged. "I'll see what I can do." She winked at him and trotted out of the room.

An hour later, Gloria brought Billy his lunch, a ham sandwich on pumpernickel bread and a little pile of raw carrots with ranch dip. Billy was familiar with ranch dip, but ham and pumpernickel were new to him. He liked them both. He also enjoyed the carrots. He had a dim recollection of eating carrots when he was very little, but he'd forgotten how sweet they were. Orange foods would be good in his diet, too, he concluded. And brown foods were going to be a must; Billy's dessert was chocolate pudding, which was the best thing he'd tasted so far in his new life. He loved chocolate. The second he tasted it, he remembered eating chocolate ice cream when he was little. How could he have gone so long without chocolate? That alone was hard to imagine.

After lunch, Gloria came to get Billy's tray. Before she picked it up, she said, "Close your eyes."

Billy blinked but complied. As soon as he did, he felt Gloria's warm hands against the sides of his head.

Something soft came down over the top of his head. Gloria's hands went away.

"Okay," she said. "Open your eyes!"

Billy opened his eyes. Gloria was holding a small mirror in front of his face. In the mirror, he saw that he was now wearing a multicolored striped hat.

"It's a Rasta beanie hat," Gloria said. "One of my coworkers crochets them."

Billy turned his head to one side and then the other. He grinned.

"This is great," he said. And it was. The hat, made of fine threads that felt lightweight and not too warm, covered his missing ears, and the bright colors made him look like he felt a lot better than he did.

"Thank you," Billy said.

Gloria patted his shoulder. "You're very welcome." She picked up his tray, waved at him, and left his room.

After Gloria left, Billy kept touching his new hat. It made him smile.

The hat had been a big surprise. But what happened next was an even bigger surprise. Billy started getting visitors.

For the three years prior to the end of his animatronic life—the three years after his mother had died—Billy had lived a pretty isolated life. Other than Maliah, his online girlfriend for just a short time, and a couple delivery people, Billy had hardly interacted with anyone. He certainly hadn't had any friends.

The new Billy, though, was going to have people in his life. This he decided after enjoying a day's worth of surprise visitors.

The first person who came to see Billy was Dr. Lingstrom.

Billy hadn't seen Dr. Lingstrom since his mom had died three years before. Dr. Lingstrom hadn't changed much in that time.

Still wearing big glasses and piling her auburn hair on top of her head in a large bun, Dr. Lingstrom's smile was wide when she rushed into Billy's room and came to his bedside to give him a hug. "I've missed you," Dr. Lingstrom said as she bent over Billy.

Unable to hug Dr. Lingstrom back because she was pinning his one arm to his side with her upper body, Billy just smiled and said, as best he could, "You too." He realized this was true. Even though he'd never really enjoyed his time with Dr. Lingstrom, and she'd never seemed to like anything he'd said or done, he felt a strange affection for the woman who used to ask him so many questions about why he wanted to be a robot. Now, of course, Billy understood that Dr. Lingstrom had been trying to help him see through his delusion. The fact that she hadn't been able to do that wasn't going to be something Billy held against her. Intuitively, Billy understood he was going to need help to be the new version of himself. He was happy Dr. Lingstrom might be around to give him that help, so much so that he even said as much.

"I want to be a new man," Billy told Dr. Lingstrom after she took a seat in the brown chair. "Can you help me with that, Dr. Lingstrom?" His lack of tongue mangled her name, but he did his best.

Dr. Lingstrom smiled widely. "I'd love to, Billy. But don't call me doctor. I won't be helping you as a doctor. You've aged out of my patient pool; I'm a child psychologist. However, I'm happy to help as a friend. You can call me Alice."

Billy frowned. That would be a tough name for him. Two of its pivotal sounds were ones he couldn't form.

Dr. Lingstrom noticed the frown. "Oh," she said. "What am I thinking?" She waved the air and laughed. "Silly me. Call me Ah-i. It will be your nickname for me."

Billy grinned. He'd never called someone by a nickname before.

The next hour was maybe the happiest hour Billy could remember since he was a little kid, and he was sorry when it was over. But after Dr. Lingstrom—no, Ah-i—left, Billy was even more surprised by his next visitors.

Some peaceful gray clouds were starting to blot out the sun when two young men, probably about Billy's age (his true age, not his animatronic age), stepped through his open doorway. Eager to meet new people, Billy looked at the men expectantly, but he didn't think he knew them.

No, wait. He did know them.

"Clark?" Billy said to the shorter of the two guys. The name came out as "Ark."

"Hey, Billy," Clark said. He gave Billy a big-toothed grin, and Billy's mind flashed to an image of a little redheaded boy pretending to be a robot in kindergarten.

Billy grinned back. "Hi, Clark."

Clark was still a redhead, but he wasn't little anymore. Short, yes, but he was well muscled; his chest was huge.

"Good to see you, Billy," Clark's companion said. "Cool hat."

"Thanks. Hi, Peter," Billy said. He laughed when he realized his version of Peter's name sounded like Pee-er. "Sorry," he continued, struggling his way through the words he wanted to say. "No tongue."

"No problem," Peter said. "We heard."

This surprised Billy. How had his old friends heard about his tongue?

Peter, who was now six foot two and lanky with a long black ponytail, pointed a finger at Billy. "You're a big deal," he said. "Everyone's talking about you."

Billy frowned. He wasn't sure he liked that idea. "Why?" he asked.

Peter walked over and dropped into the brown chair. "Are you kidding? You're the robot boy who survived being crushed."

"I'm not a robot," Billy said.

It was the first time Billy had said the words out loud, and he wasn't sure how he felt about them. Part of him was happy he no longer felt like a robot. Part of him, though, was lost without his robot self. Billy's body felt so strange to him now. Billy wasn't the animatronic he'd gotten used to being, and he wasn't the child he'd been before he'd tried to change himself. He was something in between the two, something that felt strange and incomplete.

Peter's laughter was loud in the small room. "I'm glad to hear you say that," Peter said. "You were pretty far out there for a while."

"Pete!" Clark snapped. Stepping over from the end of Billy's bed, Clark smacked Peter on the shoulder.

"What?" Peter said in mock innocence. "He was! He was in Looneyville."

For the next few minutes, they tried to one-up each other with silly names for Billy's years trying to be an animatronic. Maybe Billy should have been hurt by the teasing, but he wasn't. His friends were treating him like one of the guys. That helped him feel a little less lost and scared.

After a short visit, Billy's old friends left. Before they did, they made sure he had their phone numbers and their address. Clark and Peter were rooming together in an apartment near the local college. They were both juniors.

"Call us if you need anything," Clark said.

"We'll be back to visit you again," Peter said. "Maybe you can tell us what it was like to be a robot."

Clark swatted Peter again as the two left the room. Billy, who had smiled for most of the visit, felt his smile fade at the reminder of his lost years.

Billy would always carry the scars of his time as a would-be animatronic. Would he carry the stigma as well?

Within a few minutes of Clark and Peter's exit, Billy got two more visitors. Ned and Fran, two of the people who used to deliver groceries and other things to Billy's house, came in together.

Billy was shocked to see them. He was especially surprised to see that they'd brought a big bouquet of GET WELL balloons.

As soon as he saw the balloons, Billy remembered the rude and dismissive way he had treated Ned and Fran. Trying so hard to be a robot, Billy had been distant and aloof. And he'd never tipped them. Thinking about what a jerk he'd been, Billy blurted, "I don't deserve those."

Ned and Fran weren't able to understand Billy, so they flagged down Gloria to help. Because she'd been talking to Billy since he'd awakened, she'd gotten used to the way he spoke. She translated for Billy as he apologized to Ned and Fran for how he'd been with them.

Both of them waved away his words. "No worries," Fran, a tall, broad-shouldered woman with brown hair cut chin length, said. "We understand." She exchanged a glance with Ned. "We heard about what had happened to you, and we wanted to come and let you know we care."

Ned, who had shaggy blond hair and was as tall and broad shouldered as Fran but much heavier, looked at his big feet. Billy had a feeling Fran might have dragged Ned to the hospital.

Ned looked up. "I always felt kinda sorry for you, dude. You seemed so lonely."

Billy's eyes suddenly filled with tears. He blinked them away.

Ned was right. Billy had been lonely. He'd just never let himself face that fact. He'd used his obsession with getting his animatronic appearance right to cover how disconnected he'd felt from the world around him. And despite these visits, Billy still felt disconnected. He was the guy who'd spent sixteen years trying to be a robot. He had no tongue, no ears, and he was missing two limbs. He also had scars all over his face. Would he ever feel like he was part of the world?

Ned and Fran didn't stay long. After they left, Gloria brought Billy's dinner, spaghetti and meatballs, which Billy liked a lot. He got more chocolate pudding after that. And then he got the biggest surprise visitor of all . . . if not the most welcome one.

Billy was finishing up his pudding when he looked up and saw a short, stick-thin, stern-faced, gray-haired woman standing in his doorway. Skinny arms crossed over a crisp yellow floral blouse under a royal blue cardigan sweater that matched blue polyester slacks, Billy's grandma gazed at him with her small lips compressed.

"Grandma," Billy breathed. The word came out as "Ra-ah."

His grandma shook her head. "It's a crying shame," she said as she inspected him from head to toe.

Billy dropped the pudding cup on the tray that was pulled up to his chest. The cup started to roll across the tray's laminate surface; it headed toward the tray's edge.

Billy's grandma strode into the room and grabbed the pudding cup an inch before it would have fallen to the floor. Righting the cup, she leaned over Billy and gave him a cool-lipped kiss on the forehead.

The scents of vanilla and gardenias filled Billy's nostrils. He was immediately transported back to his childhood.

"Time for Sunday school," his grandma said, marching into his room and shaking her head at the toys scattered across the floor.

Billy's dad followed Billy's grandma into Billy's room. "He doesn't like Sunday school any more than I did, Ma," Billy's dad said.

"That's neither here nor there," Billy's grandma said. "Sunday school isn't optional."

"Did you hear what I just said?" Billy's grandma asked, extricating him from his memory.

She'd sat herself in the brown chair, and she had her knees primly together. A square pink purse sat in her lap.

Billy shook his head. "Sorry," he said. "No."

"I said I'm glad you've come to your senses." His grandma shook her head. "Maybe I should have insisted. But your mother . . ." She shook her head again. "Well, no matter. What's past is past. I'm here now."

Billy wasn't sure that was a good thing. But for the next twenty minutes, he listened politely as his grandma told him about her retirement from her job as an administrative assistant seven years before, on her seventy-fifth birthday. "I worked for as long as they'd let me," she said. "I liked the work and thought I'd hate being idle. But I've found I enjoy my peace and quiet. I keep myself busy reading, baking, painting, and puttering in my garden."

Billy wasn't sure what to say to the woman he remembered as a grumpy presence in his life. She was almost a stranger to him.

Billy hadn't seen his grandma for over fifteen years. Even though she had some of his dad's, and Billy's, own features—the round cheeks and small eyes—she felt like a stranger to him.

At the end of twenty minutes, Billy's grandma looked at her watch and stood. Gazing down at Billy, she nodded once, as if reaching a decision that she didn't share. "We'll get to know each other," she said. "You just concentrate on getting well."

And then she left. Billy let out a long, pent-up breath.

His grandma made him nervous. But it didn't matter. Overall, it had been a good day. Billy couldn't believe he'd had so many visitors. When was the last time he'd seen this many people?

Billy sat back and closed his eyes. He was worn-out from the day's excitement, and he was struggling with a tangle of emotions.

Although Billy's visitors had been a nice surprise, they'd unsettled him. Who was he now? He wasn't a robot anymore. But was he fully *Billy*? He felt like he was missing parts of himself, and he didn't know how to find them.

But even with his parts missing, Billy knew one thing: He was glad to be alive.

TALES FROM THE PIZZAPLEX

★ ★ ★

Billy had learned that hospitals weren't all that conducive to a good night's sleep. Even though his own room was dark, the nurses left the door to his room open, and a sickly greenish light spilled in through the doorway. The hospital was quiet, but Billy wasn't left in peace to sleep. Every hour or two, a nurse—not Gloria, but a rotation of three women so nondescript that Billy wasn't sure he'd have been able to describe them if asked to do so—would come in to take his pulse or give him medication.

On the third night, though, no nurses came in to bother Billy. Or maybe he was just so tired after all his visitors that he hadn't noticed when they did. Billy fell asleep quickly, and when he woke up, the clock on the wall above the nurses' station read 2:24 a.m. He'd been asleep for over five hours.

And why was he awake now?

Billy shifted positions on the bed, turning onto his right side. As he moved, he heard his name being called.

Billy froze. He lifted his head and peered out into the pukey-green light that filled the hall. No one was at the nurses' station. He heard no voices or footsteps. Where were all the nurses?

Billy started to settle back down again. But then he heard his name again, faint and eerie, almost surreal.

"Billy," a voice called, drawing out each of the letters.

The sound raised all the hairs on his body. He could feel prickles on every inch of his skin, even on the skin that was no longer there. It felt like his whole body had turned into a pincushion pierced by thousands and thousands of needles. Billy shivered as the blood began pumping through his veins faster and faster and faster.

"Biiillyyy," the voice crooned again.

Billy sat up.

Billy didn't want to sit up. What he wanted to do was curl up in a ball and pull the covers over his head. His shivers were turning into quivers that were so violent that his teeth began to chatter.

But still, Billy sat up. He also reached across his body with his right hand and lowered the rail on the left side of his bed, the way Angie had showed him.

Billy's name was called again.

He reached for the crutch that leaned against the foot of his bed and tucked it under his right arm. Billy stood, balancing his weight between his braced left leg and the crutch.

A draft from his open doorway reminded Billy that his hospital gown was flapping open in the back. He let go of the crutch, and balancing himself between his one leg on the floor and his hip against the side of his bed, he reached around with his right hand and overlapped his hospital gown, fumbling to tie it tight enough to keep the cool air out and his bare backside in. Sweating with effort, Billy then gripped his crutch again.

For several seconds, Billy held himself still, listening. Outside Billy's room, the hallway was unusually silent. The only thing Billy could hear was his own rapid breathing.

Then he heard his name again, called in the same drawn-out way, in the same hush. Billy followed it compulsively.

Although Billy could get around with one leg and the crutch, he didn't do it smoothly or quickly yet. The strain of using muscles that had been idle for a long time made his gait herky-jerky, and the exertion caused him to pant heavily.

Billy heaved himself out into the empty hallway and

blinked up at the strange green-tinged lights. They cast an unnatural glow over all the gray and white expanses that filled the hall.

Billy looked at the empty nurses' station. The station was a U-shaped white desk that contained several computers and metal filing baskets stuffed with papers. Four rolling gray desk chairs were bunched together a few feet from the desk. It had never been empty before.

Billy turned away from the abandoned nurses' station and looked up and down the hall. The linoleum floor was primarily pale gray, but a wide dusky-blue stripe ran down the middle of the hall. He had used that stripe to help him walk straight with Angie.

Every time Billy had been out in the hall with Angie, it had been busy, filled with patients shuffling along with their IV stands, visitors carrying flowers or balloons, and nurses rushing from one room's wide doorway to the next. But now Billy saw no one. The hospital was unusually still.

Now that he was out in the hallway, though, Billy realized he could hear something other than his breath. A rhythmic beeping and a whooshing sound came from a long way off, and so did the occasional scrape and thunk.

And there was his name again. "Biiillyyy."

Billy cocked his head and tried to pinpoint where that sound was coming from. He looked down; he thought the origin of the voice was under him, maybe on one of the lower floors of the hospital.

Billy looked along the length of the hall again. His gaze landed on the gray metal doors of the elevator at the end of the hall. He turned and headed that way.

While Billy concentrated on keeping his balance steady between his leg and his crutch as he followed the blue stripe down the hall, he asked himself repeatedly what he was doing. Why was he going toward a sound that was totally unnerving him? Nothing about the way his name was being used was encouraging or soothing. Billy really didn't want to face whomever was calling him. But he couldn't seem to resist the summons. It felt like it reached right into the core of him, tied itself to his will, and dragged him toward it. He had no choice but to go.

It took just a few minutes for Billy to reach the elevator. There, struggling to catch his breath, he started to prop himself against the wall so he could push the elevator button. Before he could do that, though, the elevator door whisked open.

"Biiillyyy!"

The call still seemed to be coming from below Billy. It remained faint but insistent.

Billy's heart rate went up even more when he looked into the empty, gray-carpeted, and blue-cloth-paneled elevator car. Why had the elevator stopped for him?

Billy tried to control his racing thoughts. It was weird, sure, but maybe there was a reason why the elevator had stopped. Billy stepped into the deserted car, which smelled like coffee and pine-scented cleaner. He painstakingly turned himself so he could look at the control panel.

The elevator doors made a sucking sound as they slid closed. Before Billy could decide which button to push, the elevator vibrated and began to descend. Billy frowned and looked up at the numbers above the door, watching the numbers tick down. When the L lit up, Billy expected the doors to open. He hadn't pushed a button in time, so of course it had returned to the lobby.

But the elevator kept going down. Now the number display read B1, then B2, then B3.

The elevator door whooshed open. Billy squinted against the harsh yellow light spilling into the dim elevator car's interior. The light was so glaring, he didn't notice the janitor in the olive-green uniform standing there until the janitor threw out an arm to hold the elevator door open.

"You getting out?" the heavyset, wavy-haired man asked as he repositioned a cleaning cart with a bucket, a mop, and several other maintenance supplies.

Billy nodded, and the man stepped back to give Billy room to maneuver through the open doorway. Billy was afraid the man might ask what Billy was doing down here, but he didn't. The man's expression was blank, even sleepy, as he entered the elevator, pulling the cart along with him after Billy exited. Billy got a whiff of body odor and spearmint gum when the janitor passed him.

"Biiillyyy!"

Now the voice, though still slightly muted, was clearer. Billy looked down a narrow, beige-tiled hallway.

Unlike the wide, clean hallway on the seventh floor, this one was confined and dingy. As Billy moved away from the elevator, the hall's overhead fluorescent lights dimmed. Many of them were flickering, and they all emitted a buzz that did nothing to mask the sound of Billy's name when it was sung out again.

Billy could now tell that whoever was calling him was at the end of the creepy hall. Billy could feel the pull of the voice even more strongly. He knew that it came from behind a closed brown metal door at the end of the hall.

★ ★ ★

As soon as the door clicked closed behind Billy, he sucked in his breath and let out a small whine.

"Biiillyyy."

Billy's gaze whipped toward one of the long cabinet doors on the back wall of the small room. Leaning on his crutch, he lifted his right hand and wiped sweat from his forehead. Then he regripped his crutch and took three steps forward. Stopping, he once again propped himself up with the crutch. His hand trembling noticeably, he reached for the chrome handle on the cabinet door.

Even as Billy grasped the cool metal, he could hear his own voice shouting at him in his head. Not hampered by a missing tongue, Billy's inner voice sounded the way he remembered he used to sound, and its message was crystal clear: "No! Don't open that!"

Billy knew why the wiser part of him wanted him to leave the cabinet door closed. He knew because he also now knew, with terrifying clarity, what waited for him behind that door.

Maybe Billy had known all along. Maybe he'd known the second he'd first heard his name sung.

What lay inside the long cabinet, a cabinet that looked—Billy now admitted to himself—not so much like a cabinet but more like a morgue drawer, was the other half of Billy. Even though the drawer was closed, Billy felt like he could see into it. He could see the excised part of himself—all the metal and plastic materials that he'd added, still clinging to pieces of flesh and tissue Dr. Herrera had had to remove from Billy in order to get all the robotic components out. This animatronic creation, which he'd worked so hard to embrace, was crying out to him, begging Billy to reclaim it.

Billy, however, didn't want to take back the pieces of the life he regretted living. He wanted to move on. He wanted to be Billy, the man, not B-7, the robot.

It didn't seem to matter what Billy wanted, though. His hand tugged the cabinet door open.

Suddenly, a larger hand clamped down over Billy's. The hand was hot and calloused and strong.

"What do you think you're doing in here?!" a rough voice demanded.

Billy let go of the cabinet door handle as if it had been suddenly superheated. He turned to look up into the narrowed eyes of a large dark-haired man with an imposing full beard.

"You're not supposed to be in here," the man said.

Billy wanted to slug the man for stopping him. He also wanted to hug the man for stopping him. He did neither.

He dropped his gaze to the man's dark blue uniform. A nameplate on the man's shirt pocket said he was PAUL, HOSPITAL SECURITY.

"Come on," Paul said, studying Billy's hospital gown and then lifting his gaze to give Billy's striped beanie a bemused look. "You need to go back to your room."

Billy wanted to argue, but more than that, he wanted to do exactly what Paul said. Billy nodded meekly and began to turn to follow Paul out of the little room.

As Billy turned, his gaze landed on a narrow, dark gap between the long cabinet door and the cabinet's interior. Billy had managed to open the drawer a couple inches. It remained open as the guard ushered Billy out into the hallway.

★ ★ ★

Billy's eyes shot open. He squinted into the two faint streams of light that illuminated just enough for him to make out some squat shapes. Billy clenched his fists and found his fingers curling around crisp, cool fabric. His hospital bedsheet.

Billy exhaled.

He was back in his room. One pool of light had slipped in through a seam in the room's shades and another came from the hallway. It was just a sliver, barely sneaking through the slender opening of his nearly closed door.

Why was the door nearly closed? The nurses always left it wide open.

Billy pressed his hand to his temple. His head was throbbing. So was his leg.

His expedition to the basement had definitely been more exertion than his body could handle. But he'd had to go. The animatronic had given him no choice.

Billy shuddered. Was that why he'd woken up? Had something in a dream reminded him of nearly coming face-to-face with the part of himself he was happy to be rid of?

Had the voice returned?

How much time had passed since he'd been in the basement? It couldn't have been more than an hour, not based on the darkness in his room. And his body still ached, like he hadn't had time to rest.

Billy started to roll over and pulled the covers up over his shoulders. He wanted to forget the trip to that little room with the long metal drawers. He wanted to—

Click.

Billy froze.

The clicking sound had come from within the room. It had reached out of the darkness, stretching toward Billy from a place not nearly far enough away.

And it was coming even closer.

Click, clickety-click, click-click-click.

Under the clicking, Billy could hear a slippery squelch. The sound was wet and sinister.

It sounded like something hard and unyielding was oozing through something sodden.

Click, swish, clickety-click, squish, click-click-click.

Steeling himself, Billy shifted his weight and raised his head. He peered over his bed's railing and looked in the direction of the sounds.

Billy gasped.

In the pale shaft of light coming from his slightly open door, he could see a dark, smeared trail. The trail was made up of two substances, one shiny and dark red and the other viscous and black.

Billy breathed in sharply, and his nostrils told him what he was looking at. He took in the rotting stench of human flesh and the bitter smell of motor oil.

Billy knew exactly what was slithering his way.

Maybe he'd known since he heard the first click.

He opened his mouth and screamed.

Scrabbling for his bed rail, Billy threw his leg off the bed as soon as the metal bars were out of the way. He grabbed his crutch the second his foot touched the floor, and he launched himself from his bed a half second after that.

Billy continued to scream as he flailed toward his door. Behind him, the clicking sped up. The slippery sounds got louder.

Billy smacked the door open with his crutch and surged into the hallway, bellowing at the top of his lungs.

He saw with relief that a nurse was now at the nurses' station, but he didn't stop for help. Billy knew he couldn't explain his terror quickly enough, and he couldn't risk the animatronic finding him. He hobbled down the hall as fast as he could go.

Billy didn't make it very far. As he reached the corner of the hallway, about twenty feet from his door, a security guard—a different one than the one who had found Billy in the little basement room, this one was shorter and balding—suddenly loomed in front of Billy.

"What's all the racket?" the guard asked.

Billy didn't answer him. He just attempted to keep going. He wanted to get as far from the thing in his room as possible.

The guard, however, wouldn't let Billy flee any farther. He wrapped a thick arm around Billy's waist, and when Billy started trying to use his crutch to whack the guard's leg, the guard knocked the crutch from Billy's grasp and called out, "A little help here!"

Weak from his time in bed, Billy was no match for the guard's strength. Even though he writhed in the guard's grasp, the guard easily lifted Billy off the ground.

Being picked up fired all Billy's flight-or-fight systems. He shrieked even louder, and he twisted and churned.

His panic robbed Billy of any ability to focus on his surroundings. All he could see were moving flashes of color, and all he could hear were his own caterwauls.

In the midst of this chaos, Billy felt himself being lifted even higher. Then suddenly, he was lying prone. Once he was in this position, he felt his arm being pinioned.

After that, he realized he was in motion. Whatever he was lying on was rolling down the hallway.

They were taking him back to his room!

"No!" Billy shouted. "There's something in my room!"

Unfortunately, what Billy said sounded like "Oh, hair omhing i eye oom."

Billy tried again. "Please. Don't. There's something in my room." This came out no better: "Pee, oh, hair omhing i eye oom."

Through the confusion of movement, Billy spotted a nurse's uniform. Maybe it was one of the nurses who could understand him. He zeroed in on her wide eyes, and he tried to throw her a pleading look.

Either the nurse didn't understand Billy or she didn't believe him. She did nothing to stop what was happening.

Hoarse and starting to choke on his own spittle, Billy stopped yelling. His chest heaved.

A few seconds passed in a continued blur of confusion. Then Billy felt his body land on his hard hospital bed mattress. More chaos. Billy felt something stretching across his chest and his hips. A sting bit into his arm. More pressure. Something cold pressed against his right wrist.

Then all the movement stopped. Billy blinked several times and looked around. In the light spilling into the room from the hallway, he could see that he was back in his room, alone.

Billy tried to move, but he couldn't. Lifting his head, he looked down at his body.

They'd strapped him to the bed! Billy was restrained. Not only that, whatever they'd given him was starting to make him feel woozy. His head felt heavier than it should have, and it felt like the air around him was thick and spongy. Sudden drowsiness made his eyes flutter.

The light from the hallway disappeared. Someone had closed his door. Now only the faintest glow came from the night-light above Billy's bed. It threw out a pale yellow light that barely reached the bed's railings.

Billy moaned. He squirmed, trying to loosen his bonds.

"Please," Billy said to the empty room.

He wasn't sure who he was appealing to, but it didn't matter. No one answered him. No one came to help.

Click, swish, clickety-click, squish, click-click-click.

Billy moaned again.

The thing was still here. And it was much, much closer.

"I want back in." The voice was the same one that had called Billy's name. The voice was darkly musical and raspy, contorted as if it came through a damaged synthesizer . . . which, of course, it did.

The last time Billy had spoken as B-7, he'd used the external synthesizer in his computer. A couple days before that, though, Doc had implanted a speaker in Billy's throat. The speaker had its own synthesizer, but Billy hadn't been able to get it to work before he'd broken down and fled his house.

The clicking and slippery sounds moved away from Billy's bed. They skittered into the far corner of the room and then skirred back again.

"Please," the voice wheedled. "Won't you let me back in? I've missed you so much. We were buddies, weren't we? You and me? We're supposed to be together."

Billy lay perfectly still. He didn't respond to the voice.

Something jostled Billy's bed. He stifled a gasp as he tried to raise his head so he could see the thing that spoke to him. But Billy couldn't make out what was clicking and sliding over the floor.

"Please let me back in," the voice urged again. "You need me. Look what they've done to you. It's so sad. You're tethered like an animal. I can help you if you invite me back in. Come on, B-7. We're better together. You know we are."

The clicking got louder, and the bed vibrated again. Billy strained his neck.

And there . . . he saw it!

A vaguely human-shaped metal-and-plastic head rose up above the side of Billy's mattress. Billy heard a whimper gurgle in the back of his throat as he stared at bits of bloody flesh and tissue that clung to a tangled mass of metal plates and other mechanical parts.

As grisly as the thing was, Billy couldn't stop staring at it as two of the plates parted and it spoke again. "I'm your friend, B-7," it said. "I want to help you. Everyone in your life has failed you. No one else helped you when you were alone. They only took from you. They *stole* from you. They tried to *control* you. I just want to work *with* you. We're a team."

Billy wanted desperately to block out its words. He wanted to cover his ears, but his hands were bound.

The ghastly fleshy-metal mass dropped out of Billy's view. More clicking made it clear that the thing was moving around to the other side of the bed.

"You know what you really are, B-7," the thing said as it clicked. "I only want you to be happy, and to be happy, you have to live your true life. Your true life is as an animatronic. We're meant to be together. We were designed to be as one."

Billy jerked his hand back and forth, trying to free himself. He thrashed against the strap over his chest. His efforts were futile; he couldn't get loose.

The remote control, Billy thought. He could call for a nurse. Stretching out his fingers, Billy tried to find the remote. He couldn't. It must have been out of his reach. He was helpless.

Billy was having trouble staying awake, too. Whatever they'd injected him with was working its way into his consciousness. His focus was slipping away. His senses were getting duller and duller.

"Please, B-7," the thing said. "I have your best interests at heart. You have to listen to me."

No, I don't, Billy thought. And he was right. Billy gave in to the fog that was filling his mind. Closing his eyes, he fell asleep.

Sunlight intruded into Billy's soft, gray world. The effect of it was like cold water in the face. Billy woke fully, abruptly.

Asleep one second and totally alert the next, Billy went into a panic. Feeling like he should be alarmed but not sure why, Billy's hand groped around. He found the remote that hung on the rail of his bed. He pushed the button that would call Gloria to him. She'd tell him why he felt so frightened and threatened.

Gloria was in Billy's room within seconds of his summoning her. "You poor, poor thing!" Gloria cried as she trotted toward Billy's bed. "I heard you had some excitement last night." She hurried to Billy's side and patted his shoulder.

At least Gloria was still on his side. Billy was freaked

out for reasons he didn't understand, but his freak-out level was dropping a few notches.

"What happened last night?" Billy asked. He knew something had, but he could only hold on to wisps of images. Of nightmares.

Gloria moved away from the bed and reached for the pitcher of water that sat on Billy's nightstand. "It sounds like you had a whopper of a panic attack," she said as she poured him a cup of water. She handed the cup to him.

Billy at first thought he wouldn't be able to lift his hand and take the water. He didn't know why he thought that. He'd been drinking on his own for three days.

Billy's hand came off the bed and grasped the cup of water with no trouble at all. He took a drink and handed the cup back to Gloria. Then he repositioned himself in the bed. He wasn't sure why he was so relieved that he could do that, too.

Billy frowned. Why did he think he'd gone through something more than a panic attack the night before?

Billy left the hospital the following week. His grandma brought him home.

"Last year, I fell and broke my leg," Billy's grandma said as she walked with Billy up a long wood ramp to a covered porch stretching across the front of a small yellow cottage. "That's when I had all the ramps installed. I have to say that they make it easier to get around, even now that I have two legs to use again." She glanced at Billy, who was thumping along next to her with his one leg and his crutch. "Lucky, don't you think?"

Billy, concentrating on his ascent to the porch, didn't

answer his grandma's question. Instead, he paused and looked up at the little house his grandma lived in.

Set in the middle of a wooded acre just outside town, his grandma's house was surrounded by several flower beds and many thick clusters of dark green bushes with tiny leaves. Although Billy wasn't crazy about all the flowers (*they look messy because there are too many of them*, he thought), he found the bushes and the tall evergreen trees that encircled the house to be pretty. The house itself was pretty, too. With a steep green-metal roof and two dormers, the house was like ones he'd seen in magazines—places usually described as "cozy" or "inviting." Billy supposed this house could be that. He just didn't know if he wanted to accept the invitation.

But Billy followed her inside anyway and stopped in a small slate-floored entryway. The floor was covered with a yellow-and-blue rag rug, and the entryway's walls were blanketed with daisy-motif wallpaper. Looking around, Billy remained silent.

Lately, Billy had spoken as little as possible. Ever since he'd been told that he was being placed in his grandma's care, Billy had withdrawn into himself.

Or maybe learning that he would be living with his grandma wasn't what had caused Billy's sudden desire to pull inward. Maybe it was something else. Billy had a feeling it might have had something to do with the night he couldn't remember. But then again, perhaps it didn't.

Although the first few days of Billy's new life had felt exciting and hope filled, Billy had realized that the world was way, way too big for him. Having spent the previous sixteen years living as an animatronic, Billy was pretty much clueless about how to live as a man.

A few days before, Dr. Lingstrom—no, Alice, or Ah-i—had visited Billy again, and she'd explained to him that because he'd chosen to live as a robot for so long, his personality hadn't gotten to develop naturally as most children's personalities did. He basically had lived in what his former doctor had called *a mental and emotional straightjacket.*

You may have some memories of who you were before you chose to live as an animatronic, Ah-i had said, *but those aren't enough to inform who you are as an individual. It will take a bit of time for you to figure out who Billy is, what kind of person you want to be.*

Billy's grandma stowed her purse in the drawer of a small cabinet in the entryway, and she hung up her cardigan on a mirrored oak coatrack attached to a compact bench. Turning, Billy's grandma studied him. Her gaze went to his beanie, which she'd commented on at the hospital. *Why are you wearing that silly hat?* she'd asked when she'd picked him up.

It covers my ears, Billy had told her.

Perhaps a nice simple bandanna would be better, she'd suggested.

Billy had looked at her blankly, and she'd sighed and let the subject go. Now she frowned, whether about his hat or his continued silence, Billy didn't know.

Sighing, Billy's grandma pointed straight ahead toward a short hallway. "Both bedrooms are down that hall on the right, just beyond the living room." She gestured over her right shoulder, and Billy looked into a cramped living room. Crammed full with an oversize yellow-floral sofa, a large wood rocking chair with a padded green-and-beige-striped seat cushion, a yellow wingback chair, and a simple light-colored wood coffee table and two matching end tables, the room felt stuffy. Not thrilled with the profusion of flowers outside, Billy was even less happy with all the flowery things inside. Besides the sofa's pattern, the room's yellow walls were covered in paintings or photographs of flowers, and two vases stuffed with fresh flowers sat on the end tables. Another vase filled with more flowers was perched on a thick wood mantel—maybe oak—above a pint-size brick fireplace. Billy couldn't imagine sitting in the room. It would feel claustrophobic.

In the corner of the living room, a heavily carved wood grandfather clock guarded the space. A big brass pendulum attached to a long metal rod swung back and forth inside the clock, filling the room with a *tick-tick-tick* that got on Billy's nerves. No, it was more than that. The ticking made him anxious. Why?

"The kitchen is that way, just through the dining room," Billy's grandma said, pointing to the left of the front door, toward the opposite side of the entryway from the living room. "You probably don't cook," she said. "Or do you?"

Billy knew how to cook the white foods he'd eaten as an animatronic, but he didn't want to eat those foods anymore. He figured he could learn to cook other things, but he didn't feel like explaining that to his grandma. He shrugged in answer to her question.

Billy's grandma gave him a scathing look; the expression bunched up the many wrinkles around her small mouth. Then she shrugged in return. "No matter." She stepped into a dining room barely big enough to hold a round, dark-colored wood table surrounded by uncomfortable-looking straight-backed chairs with frilly yellow seat cushions. "Come on. I'll show you the rest. It won't take long."

She led him into a galley-style kitchen with white cabinets and a yellow-and-green-striped linoleum floor. The appliances looked old-fashioned to Billy; they had rounded edges and lots of chrome.

Although his grandma's house was in a quiet area and all Billy had heard outside the house were a few birds tweeting and the wind rustling the tree branches, the inside of his grandma's house seemed noisy to him. To start with, it was filled with the big clock's endless ticking—Billy could still hear it clearly in the kitchen. It also had other intrusive sounds. The refrigerator's motor hummed loudly, and what Billy assumed was a furnace alternately rumbled and thumped.

Leaving the kitchen through a doorway on its opposite end, his grandma turned right into a small hallway and pointed at a closed door. "That's the pantry," she said. She continued on and pointed through an open doorway. "Laundry room." Then she turned right again.

Billy realized that they were coming out in the opposite end of the hallway that extended into the house from the entryway. The hall ran in a straight line from the front door to a back door next to the laundry room. They'd just done a loop, Billy realized, starting at the entryway and going through the dining room and into the kitchen to end up at the back of the hall, opposite the front door. A narrow flight of stairs went up to the left of the end of the hallway.

"That leads to the second floor," Billy's grandma said. "It's not much more than an attic. I use it for storage."

Billy peered up the stairs and nodded. Billy's grandma

turned away from the stairs and motioned for him to follow her down the main hall, heading back toward the front door. She waved a hand toward the left side of the hall. "There are just the two bedrooms and one bath between them," she said as she led Billy down the hall. "We'll have to share."

Billy nodded again.

Billy's grandma stopped in front of the first of three open doorways on the left side of the hall. "This is my room," she said.

She moved on and led Billy through the next doorway into a small room that held a double bed, a nightstand, a dresser, and a desk. The bed was covered with a plain dark green bedspread.

Billy looked around. He screwed up his face at the room's walls. They were covered with floral wallpaper—tiny yellow rosebuds in a dainty pattern. On top of the wallpaper hung framed sketches of individual flowers. He tried very hard not to sigh, and he succeeded . . . barely.

Billy was, as Ah-i had said he would be, still trying to figure out what Billy, the man, liked and didn't like. For sure, he didn't like florals.

Maybe noticing the pinched look Billy probably had on his face, his grandma said, "You can change this room to suit you." She cocked her head and studied him. "But not if you intend to make it all gray and filled with metal like that house of yours."

Billy raised his head and studied the room. How would he decorate it if he could choose? He wouldn't pick gray and metal again. That was B-7's choice. Billy was going to have to figure out what *he* liked. At least he had a place to stay while he discovered his own tastes.

"How about you take a little rest?" Billy's grandma said behind his back. "I'll bring in your things after that."

Billy turned and looked at his grandma. She raised a severely arched gray brow at Billy.

"I gathered up a few of your belongings from the house," she said, "but then I bought you some new things, too. You need color, young man."

Billy immediately felt guilt. Or was it shame? He felt bad that his eighty-two-year-old grandma was going to have to carry his possessions into the house. Billy didn't know much about how normal humans lived, but he was sure they didn't let their grandmas lift things for them.

Billy, however, could barely walk around, much less carry something. Even though Billy was no longer wearing a brace on his left leg, he still had trouble balancing on the one leg and the crutch.

Billy turned around again. He waited until he heard the bedroom door close and he could barely hear his grandma's heavy footfalls—she wore heavy-soled shoes and clomped like a person twice her size. Then he turned and crossed the bare wood floor to the bed. There, he sat and listened to the *tick-tick-tick* that went on and on and on.

Billy might not have liked his grandma much, and he didn't like the inside of her house, but he did like what she made for dinner that night. It was a red food, furthering his conclusion that he was going to want to eat a lot of red foods.

"You used to like lasagna when you were little," his grandma said as she put a thick slab of pasta layered with cheese and red sauce on a green stoneware plate in front of Billy.

Billy did still like lasagna, he discovered. It was great, so great that he finally spoke. "This is really good," he said.

His grandma tilted her head and quirked her lips for a few seconds. Then she said, "Thank you." She shook her head. "It's going to take some time for me to understand you." She pointed at his mouth. "How do you eat without a tongue?"

"Very carefully," Billy said.

His grandma barked out a gravelly laugh. It was the first time he could remember hearing her laugh . . . even in his childhood memories. He hadn't been trying to be funny; it was hard eating without a tongue. He had to concentrate to make sure he didn't get things stuck in his throat.

After they finished their lasagna, his grandma gave him a slice of chocolate cake. The cake confirmed what he'd concluded about chocolate: It was his new favorite thing.

After the cake, his grandma asked if he wanted to play checkers. He told her he didn't know how. So, she taught him.

Checkers were okay, Billy thought. It was fun to play a game. Billy, however, decided he preferred video games.

After the game, Billy went to his room. His grandma had left his possessions on the floor by the door. He pushed them with his crutch over to the end of his bed. There, he sat down and went through them. He didn't find much that mattered to him.

His grandma had only brought from Billy's house a couple items of his old gray clothing. (The vibrant colors of the shirts she'd bought to go with a couple pairs of new jeans made it clear what she thought of gray.) The rest of what was in the box was toiletries and a few books.

Billy frowned. Where was his computer?

Standing, Billy went to his bedroom door. He opened it and called out, "Grandma!"

Clomping sounded above Billy's head. Then it came down the stairs.

"What is it, Billy?" his grandma asked. She had a smudge of red paint on her cheek.

The red looked like blood. It made Billy uneasy.

"Where is my computer?" Billy asked.

His grandma shook her head. "You don't need a computer. All that digital stuff is part of what got you in trouble in the first place. That and TV."

The mention of TV made Billy realize that he hadn't seen one in his grandma's house. "Where is your TV?" he asked. Maybe it was in her bedroom, and he just hadn't spotted it.

She shook her head. "Don't have one. Filled with all kinds of nonsense, TV. Like that show that started all your troubles to begin with."

No computer. No TV.

"Before you ask, I don't have a cell phone, either," Billy's grandma said.

Billy raised his eyebrows and stared at his grandma. "No cell phone?!"

"Good gracious, no! Infernal things," his grandma said, after she took a few seconds to figure out what he'd said.

Who didn't have a cell phone? Billy thought. Everyone had a cell phone.

"I have a good old rotary phone in my bedroom," his grandma said as if reading his thoughts. "That's enough for me."

Billy shook his head. "I'm going to bed," he said.

He needed to be alone. He needed to think.

"Sweet dreams," his grandma said. She watched him make a painstaking turn. Then she looked away from him.

Closing his bedroom door behind him, Billy leaned against it and shook his head. No computer. No TV. No cell phone. Nothing but too many flowers and a clock that wouldn't shut up.

Billy hadn't exactly lived a busy life as an animatronic, but his days hadn't been filled with silence. He'd nearly always been online when he was a robot. He'd spent lots of time on social media. He'd played online games and he'd watched hours of videos and done research on the internet. His brain had been constantly stimulated. He was going to lose his mind in this house.

I'd be happier in the hospital, Billy thought. *At least they have TV.* Tomorrow morning, Billy decided, he'd tell his grandma he wanted to go back to the hospital.

Billy wanted to go now, but he knew it was late, and demanding to be taken back tonight would be rude. Even his newly developing human self understood that.

Feeling better for having made his decision, Billy slowly got ready for bed. One of the things that his grandma had bought him was a pair of burgundy-red pajamas. He put those on, went out into the hall, and headed toward the bathroom

Billy didn't hear his grandma moving around. She must have been in her bedroom, but if she was, she was silent. All Billy could hear was the refrigerator's hum, the furnace's rumble, and the *tick-tick-tick* of the grandfather clock.

Billy went into the bathroom. After using the toilet, he brushed his teeth. Then he noticed he had a smudge of lasagna sauce on his jaw. The streak reminded him of the paint he'd seen on his grandma's face. Like the paint, the sauce looked like a smear of blood.

Billy's hand started to shake. Trying to steady it, he reached for a washcloth and got it wet. When the wet terry cloth slid over the edge of the sink, Billy's breath caught in his throat. Behind the slippery sound, the *tick-tick-tick* of the clock suddenly sounded even louder than usual.

Billy's breath started coming out in little gasps. His leg went weak. He sank down onto the closed toilet seat.

I remember.

He wished he didn't.

Sweat beaded on Billy's forehead and chills wracked his body. He felt like someone was pushing on his chest.

I can't go back to the hospital, Billy thought. If Billy was in the hospital, B-7 would find him.

Billy took a deep breath and managed to find the strength to stand. Picking up the washcloth, he cleaned off his face. Then he returned to his room.

As Billy got under the crisp yellow sheets beneath the green bedspread, he heard a muffled trill. Billy froze and listened. The deep jangle started to repeat but was cut off. Billy realized he was tense, and he shook his head at his overreaction. It was just his grandma's old rotary phone, he realized. Billy exhaled and settled in bed.

Lying back on the pillows, Billy tried to ignore the relentless ticking of the grandfather clock. He closed his eyes and blotted out the flowers looking down at him from every wall in the room.

Billy might not have liked it here, but he had to stay. Until he had his strength back and had uncovered more of who Billy the person was going to be, he would be safer in this little country cottage, even with all its flowers and ticking. Here, he was not only far away from the hospital, he was far away from his old body. And he wanted to keep it that way.

Once he decided that his grandma's house was the best place for him to be, Billy made a concerted effort to get used to the flower-filled home with the ticking clock. One thing Billy had learned from looking back at his life as an animatronic was that he was good at immersing himself in a role. His role now was "dutiful grandson," so he put all his energy into that.

Within a few days of moving in, Billy had a routine going. In the morning, he had coffee with his grandma at the round table in the dining room. She got up before dawn every morning and baked, so by the time Billy was up, about 7 a.m., there were muffins or pastries or coffee cake to go with the rich, dark coffee. Eating his grandma's baked goods, Billy learned quickly that he'd been severely depriving himself of pleasure during the years he'd stuck to white foods.

When they sat with their coffee, Billy and his grandma rarely spoke. He always had to concentrate to eat or drink without making a mess, and his grandma liked to do the crossword puzzle in the morning paper. The silence, though strained for a couple of days, quickly started feeling comfortable, and Billy began feeling a fondness for the old lady with the perpetually sour expression. She seemed to be warming to him as well. She'd stopped making comments about his striped beanie hat, and she no longer stared at his scars and missing limbs. She didn't sigh and frown around him anymore, and her quick responses to whatever he said to her indicated that she was getting used to the way he spoke.

Although the grandfather clock's ticking continued to pester Billy like a bothersome splinter under his skin, he started feeling better about it after his grandma explained that the clock had been made for her great-great-great-great-great-great-grandfather as payment for his services—he'd been a doctor. It had been passed down through the family for over two hundred years.

"When I'm gone," Billy's grandma told him, "I want it to go to your dad."

"Where is my dad?" Billy asked. He hadn't thought about his dad in a very long time. After his dad had left, Billy, as B-7, had found that it was best to wipe away any thoughts about his dad. It hurt less.

Billy's grandma shook her head. "I haven't heard from him in a year or so. Last time he sent me a letter, he was somewhere in Peru, working for one of those companies harvesting the rain forests." Billy's grandma sighed, and he knew she wasn't happy with Billy's dad.

After a couple minutes of silence, during which Billy and his grandma watched the grandfather clock's pendulum swing back and forth, his grandma said, "Anyway, this clock will be yours someday."

Then she showed him how to wind the clock so it kept going. This became part of Billy's regular routine, and he found that he developed affection for the clock. The ticking, after that, became more soothing than irksome.

After breakfast and clock winding, Billy had other duties in the house. His grandma's baking created a lot of dirty dishes, and she had no dishwasher, so it became Billy's task to clean up the bowls and pans that she used.

This was a tricky operation, given that Billy had just the one hand to use and the one leg to prop himself on, but after a couple days of getting the hang of it, he became adept at one-handed dishwashing, and his left leg got stronger and stronger. In addition to washing dishes, Billy took on dusting. He also became what his grandma called her "fix-it man." When Billy had been an animatronic, he'd learned to do household repairs. He was adept at dealing with electrical and plumbing issues. His grandma's old house had plenty of those, so that kept him busy.

In the afternoons, his grandma took a nap. While she was sleeping, Billy would sit in her rocking chair in the living room. The chair sat next to the picture window, which looked out over the front porch and beyond it to the thick, bright foliage providing a buffer between the house and the narrow country lane that led into town. Having gotten used to the crowded living room, so much so that it felt comfy now instead of cramped, Billy sat in the rocking chair to read, but he often looked outside. When he used his foot to rock the chair, he enjoyed the way the motion calmed him as he watched little gray birds flitting around in the bushes.

After Billy's grandma got up from her nap, they would have "tea." Tea wasn't actually tea. It was usually more coffee or sometimes hot chocolate, and they had it out on the front porch, no matter how chilly it was outside.

Fresh air is important, Billy's grandma had said the first time she told Billy to "bundle up" so they could sit outside and have their "tea." *The cold air will put color in your cheeks.*

Billy and his grandma sat together on the white porch swing every afternoon. They would sip their coffee or hot chocolate, steaming in thick, squat mugs, and they'd work together, unconsciously, to get the swing swaying back and forth. Billy decided his body liked to be rocked. The sensation made him feel safe and relaxed.

In the evenings after dinner, Billy and his grandma played games. Besides checkers, she taught him to play several other games—dominos, Chinese checkers, Monopoly, and Scrabble. Although checkers didn't engage Billy much, he liked the rest of the games. He especially enjoyed Scrabble. He found he was good at it, probably because of all the reading he'd done as an animatronic. His grandma was good at it, too—they had close-matched games that they both enjoyed.

In spite of the slow pace of life at his grandma's house, Billy was tired at the end of the day. He was always ready for bed before nine. Each night, he'd slide under the covers exhausted, and as he settled in, he'd often hear, as if from a great distance, the deep ring of his grandma's phone. Billy idly wondered who was calling, but it wasn't any of his business.

On the first Sunday that Billy lived with his grandma, five days after he moved in, their morning routine changed. When Billy got up, his grandma told him to put on a "good shirt and slacks," both of which she'd bought for him, because they were going to church.

The idea of church made Billy think of the Sunday school classes of his childhood, and he wasn't enthused about going, but he'd already learned that living with his grandma meant doing what she wanted him to do. Still, he was nervous about going to church. There would be people there—people who would stare at him and whisper about him.

When Billy had been B-7, he hadn't cared when others had stared, pointed, or talked about him. The fact that others hadn't understood him had been irrelevant to him. Robots had no interest in the opinions of others.

Billy, the man, however, *did* care about what others thought. Even after he started getting visitors in the hospital, Billy had been self-conscious about his scars and his missing ears and tongue and limbs. He knew that his life as B-7 was something other people didn't understand. In fact, even Billy understood it less and less as the days went by.

When Billy and his grandma walked through double doors into the small hundred-year-old wood church with the jutting steeple and the old bell that was ringing when they arrived, Billy discovered that he needn't have worried about what people would do or say around him. Only thirty-seven people sat in the wood pews that day (Billy counted them), and every one of them treated Billy like he was just an ordinary guy. No one stared or pointed. No one whispered about him. No one cared that he was missing pieces or that he'd lived most of his life as a robot. He was accepted immediately.

The service in the little church wasn't anything like the Sunday school classes Billy had hated. No one made him memorize anything or stand up and recite anything. All he had to do was sit in the pew next to his grandma and listen to the pastor, a kind-faced man with white hair that flopped over one of his friendly blue eyes. After the sermon, they sang hymns. Billy hadn't liked singing in Sunday school and church services when he was little, but now the singing surprisingly put him at ease, perhaps because of all he'd been through.

When the service was over, several people came over to say hi to Billy. Everyone seemed very happy to meet him and didn't bat an eye at the way he spoke.

"Do you like to fish, Billy?" one man with a pointy goatee and a large belly asked. Billy's grandma introduced the man as Frank, and she said he made the best pickles she'd ever tasted.

"I don't know," Billy said. "I've never been fishing."

"Well," Frank said, clapping Billy on the shoulder. "We'll have to remedy that. There's a good fishing spot not far from here that's easily accessible. I'll take you next Sunday after church if you'd like."

Billy didn't know if he'd like fishing, but he liked Frank. So, he nodded. "That would be great," he said.

Billy was practically floating when he and his grandma got home from church. He couldn't stop grinning.

Seeing his expression, his grandma grinned back at him, but she didn't ask about why he was happy. All she said was, "Go change your clothes, then we'll have Sunday dinner."

That evening, Billy went to bed earlier than usual. The day had been good, but being around people had sapped his strength.

After Billy got into bed, he closed his eyes and thought about his day. For the first time, Billy felt like he could go forward without beating himself up for the bad choices he'd made, for all the lost time, and for all the damage he'd done to himself. Billy knew he still had a long way to go to understand who "just Billy" was, but at least he now felt like he had a clean slate to work with.

Smiling, Billy rolled onto his side and burrowed farther under the covers. Sleepiness started to quiet his mind. Just as he was drifting off, he heard the ring of the old rotary phone. Something about the ring unsettled him, but he was too tired to figure out why. As the ringing stopped, he fell asleep.

The following week passed the same way the first one had. Billy found that the simple, quiet days suited him more than he'd thought they would. On some level, he was aware that the life he was living now wasn't typical for a guy his age, but he didn't care. He didn't think he'd want to live in the country forever, but for now it was just what he needed. It was giving him time to figure out what he did want to do.

The daily routine was soothing, except for those few seconds at the end of the day as he was settling into bed. The ringing phone was bothering him more each time he heard it. *Why am I concerned about it?* he wondered. Was it the regularity of the calls? Was it the fact that his grandma never mentioned them? But then, why would she? She wasn't obliged to tell him about everything she was doing.

The second Sunday that Billy and his grandma went to church, Frank took Billy fishing afterward. Billy learned that fishing was kind of boring, but he did like sitting in a folding chair next to a river, shooting the breeze with Frank.

Billy had been a little nervous about spending time with someone he didn't know. What would he say? But Frank was easy to talk to. An author who wrote private-eye novels, Frank was really interesting and intelligent. He talked about his work in a way that made it sound like it was a lot of fun to make up characters and stories, so much so that by the time they were done fishing, Billy had decided maybe he'd like to be an author.

When Billy had been growing up, he hadn't thought about what he was going to do as an adult. He was a robot. That was all there was to what he was going to do. Since he'd started his new post-B-7 life, trying to imagine what he'd do for the rest of his days had been way too much to contemplate. The time with Frank, however, showed Billy a future he thought he might really enjoy. With two limbs missing, Billy knew his options were a little limited, but he could write.

"What should I do if I want to be a writer?" Billy asked Frank as they gathered up their fishing gear and walked away from the river.

"Write," Frank said. He guffawed, but then he sobered. "Seriously, kid," he said, "it's a cliché, but writers write. If you want to get good at any craft, you have to practice. So just start writing."

When they got back to Frank's old red SUV, Frank dug around in the back seat and pulled out a plain, lined notebook. "I use these. I have cases of them."

Frank handed the notebook to Billy. Billy took it and ran his hand over the smooth cover.

"Start keeping a journal. Write whatever comes to mind," Frank said.

And Billy did. Writing became as much of his routine as spending time with his grandma. His days became happily predictable, with two exceptions.

The first exception was a good one. Every passing day, things got better and better between Billy and his grandma. Billy even discovered that his grandma had a fun side.

The day after Billy went to church for the first time, his grandma asked him to help her in her flower garden. Still not a fan of flowers, and still struggling to get around on one leg, Billy wasn't real keen on the idea, but he decided that dutiful grandsons helped their grandmas in the garden, so he went along with it.

Luckily, his grandma had little stools for them to sit on while they worked. "I don't get up and down so easily anymore, either," she said when she brought out folding stools that had sturdy metal handles to help with getting up and down. "I've been using one of these for years," she said. "I bought a second one for you."

Billy was touched by her thoughtfulness. "Thank you," he said. He sat down and learned how to pull weeds and deadhead the flowers.

They worked in silence for a bit, and then his grandma asked, "What do you call it when a flower goes on a date with another flower?"

Confused, Billy stopped working and looked at his grandma.

"A budding romance," she said. And then she laughed her gravelly laugh.

Billy laughed, too. He hadn't known his grandma could tell a joke.

"What do you call flowers who are close friends?" he asked his grandma.

She raised an eyebrow at him. Her usually cinched-tight mouth stretched out in a smile. "What?" she asked.

Billy had a feeling she knew what he was going to say, but she let him say it. "Buds," he said.

They laughed together.

After that, Billy started liking flowers.

The second exception to the pleasurable routine of Billy's passing days was his increasing disquiet regarding the mysterious nightly phone call.

It rang at precisely 9:03. The phone never rang more than twice. Usually, the second ring was cut off.

Tonight, Billy was getting ready for bed a little later than usual. At 9:03, when the phone rang, he was just leaving the bathroom. When the ring cut off, Billy paused and listened. For the first time, he heard his grandma speaking to whomever had called.

Billy took a couple quiet steps toward his grandma's bedroom door. He could only just barely hear his grandma's voice. She wasn't talking in her normal tone. She spoke in a whisper that told Billy she didn't want him to hear the conversation, so Billy returned to his room.

The next morning when he woke, Billy thought about what he'd heard the night before. Already on edge about the phone calls, Billy found that his grandma's hushed tone added to his unease. He tried to tell himself that a regular phone call wasn't a big deal, but he thought it was strange that the call came at the exact same time each night. It was strange enough that Billy really wanted to know who his grandma was talking to. Accordingly, Billy decided he would time his pre-bed routine so he'd be in the hall again at the time of the call. This time, he'd try harder to listen in.

He tried, but he couldn't make out her whispers. Each failed attempt at eavesdropping raised Billy's anxiety. Who was calling? Why 9:03? And why the whispering? What didn't Billy's grandma want him to hear? Billy wrote in his journal about these questions, but he didn't reach any conclusions.

For over a week, even as he wrote about them, Billy told himself that the calls were none of his business. He should just ignore them. One night, though, his curiosity made him a little bolder when he listened by his grandma's door. Instead of just standing by the door, Billy put the side of his head to the paneled wood. Shifting his beanie so his ear canal was open to receive as much as possible, Billy listened hard.

His grandma's whispered words were still too muted to hear. She was definitely talking to someone because there were pauses in the whispering, as if she was listening to whomever was on the other end of the line.

Even though Billy knew it would have been wrong, he wished his grandma had a second phone in the house, so he could have picked up another receiver and listened in. Something about the call's peculiar specific timing and his grandma's whispers were making him uneasy. These weren't normal "just called to chat" phone calls. Something was going on. Billy was becoming sure of it. But what could he do about it?

Over the next couple weeks, Billy got stronger and stronger. The residual pain from his surgeries had all but disappeared, and he'd learned to do pretty much everything he needed to do to take care of himself. He also was starting to get a sense of himself. He felt like he was ready to be on his own.

Billy had surprisingly enjoyed the time with his grandma, but all the writing he was doing made him realize that if he was going to become an author, he needed to broaden his horizons. He needed some life experience beyond living in a country cottage, even beyond living in this town. Billy was so eager to get out into the world and explore, he even started looking into getting new prosthetics. Ah-i, who'd been coming out to visit Billy once a week, had brought him the information he needed to make his decision, and Billy had made arrangements to go for it.

On a chilly Thursday evening, after sharing a dinner of beef stew and corn bread with his grandma, Billy decided it would be his last night with her. He didn't tell her that; he would tell her in the morning. Billy didn't think she'd be upset. Even though they were getting along great, his grandma seemed like she was becoming tired, as if maybe his presence in her home was starting to wear on her. She was moving more slowly, and she was paler than she'd been when she'd first brought him home.

His grandma went into her room early that night. That was fine. Billy wanted to do some writing anyway.

For an hour or so, Billy wrote in his journal. By then, he was on his third notebook. (Frank had brought a stack of them to church the week after they went fishing.) Just before nine, Billy got up to step out into the hall. He was still determined to try to figure out what the 9:03 phone calls were about. So, he made sure he was near his grandma's bedroom door by 9:02.

Billy waited in the hall for a minute. When the phone didn't ring, he checked his watch. It was 9:03. He still waited. 9:04. The phone didn't ring.

Billy frowned at his watch and looked at his grandma's door. That's when he realized that he could hear her talking. Not whispering. Actually talking.

Who was she talking to?

"Grandma?" Billy called out softly.

His grandma didn't respond. She just kept talking.

Without thinking, Billy reached out and grasped his grandma's door handle. He turned it and pushed the door open. Realizing he was being impolite but not caring, Billy stepped into his grandma's bedroom.

Billy hadn't been sure of what he thought he'd see when he intruded into his grandma's space. His grandma talking on the phone? A secret romantic caller? Something else? Whatever that something else might have been, Billy never would have guessed it would be what he saw when he looked toward his grandma's bed. If he'd guessed, he never would have opened the door.

Simultaneously, Billy's breath stopped and his heart rate tripled. For several long seconds, he couldn't even move enough to inhale or exhale as he listened to his pulse pound in his ears. All Billy could do was stare at his grandma, which meant that he was also staring at the thing that had come into his hospital room and terrorized him with its exhortations to let it back in.

Billy's body demanded that he take a breath. He opened his mouth and spasmodically gulped in air. The sound he made was loud in the room, but neither his grandma nor the horrible thing creeping over her noticed the noise.

Accordioned into a pleated mass of metal and plastic, the thing, still stained with Billy's blood and encrusted with now-drying bits of Billy's tissue, was inching its way up Billy's grandma's prone body. Every move it made emitted the clicks and squelches that Billy recognized from that night in his hospital room.

His grandma, dressed in her usual combo of floral blouse and polyester pants, today's in pinks and purples, made no attempt to get away from the hideousness that was attempting to fuse itself with her. In fact, she was encouraging it. That was the talking Billy had heard.

"That's it," Billy's grandma was saying. "I know you've been alone in the dark. You've been so lonely since Billy rejected you. That's why you called, right? I'm sorry I couldn't let you be with Billy again, but we've been bonding, haven't we? You don't have to be alone anymore."

The conglomeration of parts surged upward. It latched onto a polyester-encased leg, and part of its metal sunk into Billy's grandma's skin.

Expecting his grandma's scream, Billy winced and started to rush forward. But his grandma didn't scream. She just kept talking. There was a strain in her voice, a breathiness that made it clear she was in pain, but her words were clear.

"Good," she said. "I'm so happy you're here."

His mouth open in shock, Billy watched as the thing completely took over his grandma's leg. No, not "took over." Replaced. His grandma's leg fell away from her body as the thing attached itself to her hip and kept stretching out farther, reaching outward and upward to supplant even more of his grandma.

As it moved, the crimping and shifting metal and plastic continued to make its signature clicking and sliding sounds. Those sounds were the stimulus that finally got Billy in motion.

Angry with himself for not going to his grandma's aid sooner, Billy started rushing toward her bed. That's when his grandma noticed him.

Turning her head toward Billy, his grandma, seemingly unconcerned that her other leg was dropping away from her body, called out, "Stop!"

Billy wanted to convince himself that she was talking to her attacker, but he'd seen enough to understand that she didn't see the thing as an attacker. Billy knew she was talking to him.

"Stay away, Billy," his grandma said. "I want this. I'm ready to embrace this new life."

Billy was unwilling to accept what he was hearing. Totally repulsed by what he was seeing and compelled to stop it, no matter what his grandma said, Billy took another step.

"No, Billy," his grandma choked out, her voice tight. "Let it happen." She looked away from Billy, back down the length of her ruined body.

Billy let out a mewl of despair. How could he just stand here and watch his grandma possessed—and mutilated—by this metal and plastic creature, a creature that Billy, in essence, had created with his obsession and stupidity? Billy loathed what he'd been and what his existence had left behind. He couldn't bear to see the detritus of B-7 take the grandma he'd only just come to love.

As if in response to Billy's revulsion, the mechanical monster, now overtaking Billy's grandma's torso and working its way up an arm, turned a headlike metal protrusion woven from plastic projections, a tangle of wires, and sharp metal plates. Two of the plates parted, creating a mouthlike gap in the continually churning parts.

"I wanted to be with you, B-7," the thing said to Billy. "That's where I'm supposed to be, but you wouldn't invite me back in. I sought out your grandma so I could be close to you through her."

Billy didn't care what the writhing accumulation of metal and plastic had to say. What he cared about was that the thing had almost completely lay claim to his grandma. Its sharp edges were impaling his grandma's flesh, puncturing the skin between her ribs and burrowing deep into her torso. The thing was splicing open her sides, reaching past her bones, laying claim to her most vital organs.

The metal and plastic invader was now almost 90 percent consolidated with his grandma's body. Three of her limbs had been severed. They lay on her bed, oozing blood, but not as much blood as Billy might have expected. It was like the mechanical interloper had cauterized Billy's grandma's flesh as it had usurped it.

Rendered weak by the shock of what he was seeing and helpless by what his grandma had asked of him, Billy stood still. He wanted to look away from his grandma, but he couldn't. His gaze was riveted on her.

That's why Billy noticed when the mass of parts started to twitch. The vibration was subtle at first, but it quickly became more violent. In a matter of seconds, the wreckage of B-7 was quaking so hard that the bed's box springs squealed in protest.

What's happening? Billy wondered. It almost looked like the thing was trembling in fear.

Billy's grandma let out what sounded like a whoop of triumph. With her one remaining hand, she gripped onto the few metal and plastic parts that hadn't yet bonded themselves to her. The parts jolted, as if trying to resist, but Billy's grandma held on. She even smiled.

Raising her head to look down the length of her now-maimed body, Billy's grandma said, "You understand now, yes? Well, I'm afraid it's too late to change your mind. You're stuck with me."

Billy's grandma turned to look at Billy again. She kept hold of the parts that kept trying to flail away from her as she said, "I've been terminal for some time now, dear. I didn't say anything because I didn't want to worry you." She looked back down at the creature that was fighting to free itself from her. She bared her teeth in a strained grin. "Our friend here, though, should be *very* worried."

Billy felt a sob well up. His eyes filled with tears.

His grandma returned her gaze to Billy. "Don't waste your tears on me. I've had a good life. I'm ready for this." She grimaced as she wrestled with the still-thrashing metal and plastic. "This morning, I woke up and knew today was my last day. I want to do this one last thing."

The ex-B-7 creature's metal parts lashed in a clear frenzy to escape. "B-7, help me," it called out.

The pitiful appeal revolted Billy. He hugged himself with his one arm as the thing's clicking sounds came out faster and faster, becoming a rapid-fire din that filled the bedroom. The collection of metal discards fought furiously to free itself from Billy's grandma, but its efforts weren't enough. Billy's grandma's intention was too strong. She forced the last of the parts to meld with her arm, and she exhaled in relief as that arm spilled away from her body.

Still holding Billy's gaze, his grandma said, "Don't grieve for me. It's time for you to live. Have a good life. Be true to yourself and be kind to other people." Her face now deathly pale, Billy's grandma swallowed and licked her lips. Then she winked at Billy. "And go to Sunday school." She gave Billy a small smile.

Billy felt tears slide down his cheeks as his grandma let out one last, long exhale. She went still.

Remaining rooted, Billy continued to stare at the macabre composite of his grandma and the still-convulsing B-7 parts. The metal and plastic were moving weakly now, and with every second that Billy watched them, they slowed.

Finally, the mechanical monster stopped moving completely. The clicking ceased.

Billy looked from his grandma's staring eyes to the rigid motionlessness of the metal and plastic parts. He could see that it was over. Both his grandma and what was left of B-7 were dead.

When it was all over, Billy wanted to just leave his grandma's house and forget he'd seen what he'd seen. He couldn't, however, leave her like that. So, he sat with her for the rest of the night, and in the morning, he used the rotary phone to call Frank.

Frank helped Billy bury his grandma . . . and the dregs of B-7. He then drove Billy to the hospital so Billy could start the process of getting his new prosthetics.

"I'll be sure her house is taken care of for as long as you need," Frank told Billy as Billy got out of the old SUV.

"Thank you," Billy said as he balanced on the crutch that he expected he wouldn't need for much longer.

Billy stepped back. Frank leaned out and gave Billy a long look.

"Go forth and have adventures, young man," Frank said. "You have to experience life to write something interesting."

Billy nodded and lifted his hand to wave as Frank drove away. Then Billy made his way into the hospital.

Two weeks later, Billy walked out of the hospital without his crutch. He now sported two new prosthetic limbs; his new arm and leg were the latest in flesh-colored, real-looking prosthetics, and Billy had gotten used to them quickly.

Striding away from the hospital and wearing jeans and a new bright red shirt that went great with his striped beanie (into which Billy had tucked a small carnation—a tribute to his grandma), Billy thought about the first adventure he intended to have. He'd been living with Clark and Peter while he went through the process of being fitted for his prosthetics. It had been great to hang with them and get to know a few other guys, but he intended to stay with them for just one more night. It was time for him to get on with his life.

Not at all sure whether he was making the right choice but feeling like it was something he had to do, Billy bought a plane ticket to Lima, Peru. He intended to try to find his dad.

Both terrified and hopeful, Billy was ready to throw himself into the unknown. He wasn't sure how the trip would unfold. Maybe it would be good, maybe not. But either way, he figured he'd end up with a life experience worth writing about.

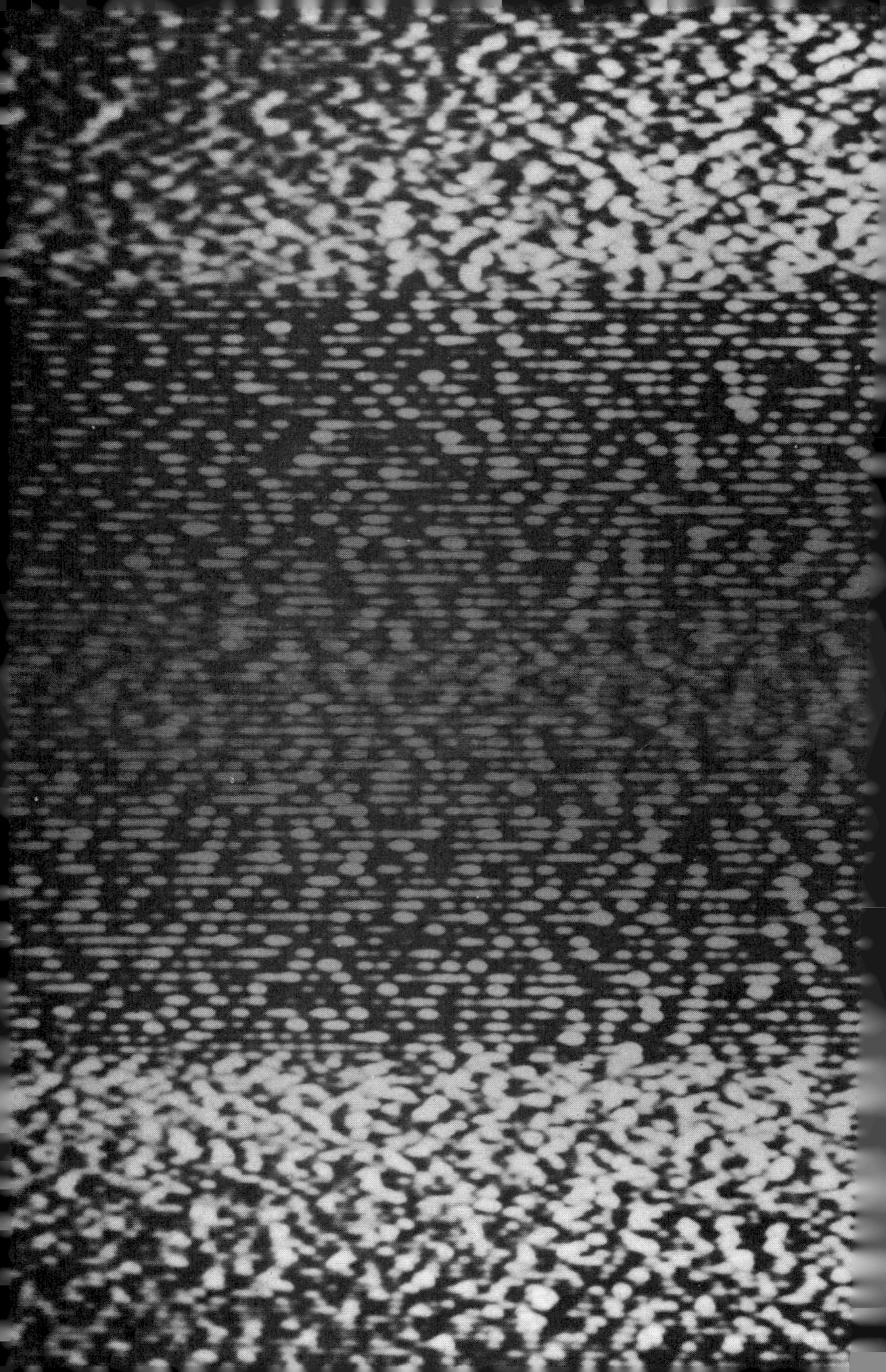

ALONE TOGETHER

TRAVIS HUTCHINS SHOVED HIS MATH BOOK INTO HIS SCHOOL LOCKER. IT WAS IN BETWEEN THIRD AND FOURTH PERIOD AT BRIGHTON MIDDLE SCHOOL. KIDS CHATTED IT UP WITH THEIR FRIENDS AS THEY WALKED BY HIM WHILE, AS USUAL, HE STOOD BY HIMSELF IN THE MAIN HALLWAY.

"Let's go to the volleyball game this Friday!"

Travis turned his head toward a kid named Pedro, who was two lockers down talking to his two friends.

"It'll be cool to all go together. Let's ask Donna and her friends to go, too."

Travis had a fleeting thought that he could say something and try to get an invite. But his jaw remained tightly closed. He'd always been a shy kid who liked to work with his hands and found it hard to make new friends. Especially in middle school.

He was an average seventh grader, with honey blond hair, who liked to wear faded tees and jeans, and hadn't quite had his growth spurt yet, which resulted in him being the shortest kid by an inch or more. He always wore his favorite Little League hat that was faded and frayed, with a little hole on the bill, for comfort.

"Yeah, that'll be fun," a kid named Brett said. "Then we could hang out at the Mega Pizzaplex afterward. So? Who's gonna ask Donna?"

Travis had seen the Mega Pizzaplex, of course. It was huge. But he'd never been inside. It wasn't the kind of place his dad would go, and he'd hoped to go with friends. If he could make them.

"Pedro should since it's his idea," Marcus suggested with a big smile.

"Fine, fine. *I'll ask*. It's not a big deal." Pedro shrugged uncomfortably, and his friends laughed.

Travis could have asked Donna. She was in his fifth-period science class. But he couldn't bring himself to jump into the conversation. His shoulders slumped as he slammed his locker shut—too hard. *Oops.*

The boys turned to look at him. Travis swallowed past the sudden tightness in his throat and shrugged at them. He felt his cheeks burn red and he tried to say sorry, but his lips wouldn't move. The boys gave him a squinty frown, and Travis ducked his head as they turned and walked away.

"So weird," he heard them whisper as they disappeared down the hall.

Travis felt a funny pressure in his chest as he adjusted his ball cap, hitched his backpack onto one shoulder, and strode down the hallway toward woodshop class with his head down. The gray-and-white-speckled floor tiles were a comforting view. Better than looking at kids who ignored him, he supposed. When Travis would see a pair of feet come into his view of the floor, he simply shifted and walked around them. The fewer awkward interactions, the better.

He liked to envision a clear bubble around him as he walked, as if no one could break through the barrier and he was protected from the put-downs and static energy from other kids that were sometimes too hard for him to be around.

He ignored the whispers, the laughs, the loud voices, and the vividly painted posters on the walls for school events and club meetings. Crowds of outgoing kids made him feel uncomfortable and out of place. He never knew how to join into conversations, and his gawky silence always made him break out in sweats.

Travis had always been shy, but he'd had a couple of friends in elementary school. But everything had changed drastically when his mom left.

His dad had withdrawn and was hardly speaking to him, and Travis had grown even quieter. Dad left for his mechanic shop early, and they ate dinner in silence when he came home. And without a parent to encourage him to sign up for band or Boy Scouts, Travis had slowly pulled out from school activities and drifted away from his old friends. He'd been so sad and hadn't known how to pretend that things were okay when they really, really weren't. So now, several years later, he was still alone.

It had changed everything.

There were times Travis blamed himself.

He blinked the painful thoughts away as he walked into the large woodshop building. The ceiling was tall and the windows were large, allowing the sunlight to shine into the substantial space. Worktables lined the center of the room and off to the side stood the big machines: the planers and tabletop saw. The room was surrounded with storage cabinets and shelves, stacked with wood, small hand tools, nails, screws, glue, rags, sandpaper, and wood stain. Travis's mood shifted as he breathed in the earthy and industrial smell of the shop. It always made him feel at ease. Secure.

In woodshop there was nothing to worry about. It was his place to create. When he created, everything in his life, even his feelings, quieted down. He enjoyed losing himself in building things from wood scraps. It made him forget that his mom was gone and that his life was lonely. He knew he didn't belong at school, but as soon as he stepped into woodshop, everything else faded away. He guessed he got his love of working with his hands from his dad. Dad worked with cars, and Travis liked to work with wood.

His father used to work with him on his school projects.

Of course that was before Mom had left.

Mr. Middlefield was at the head of the class, cleaning off his worktable and scattering small pictures around the tabletop. The bell rang and he looked up at Travis.

TALES FROM THE PIZZAPLEX

"You know the rules. Hats off in class, please."

Travis nodded and added his hat to those already on hooks by the door. Travis ran a hand through his flat hair and strode back to his table near the back.

Mr. Middlefield was his favorite teacher. He was a stout, older man with thinning gray hair and a puffy beard. He wore faded overalls and a tool belt that held a few tools and broken pencils. Each time he needed a pencil, he'd reach into his tool belt and find the tip broken off or the pencil cracked in two. He'd say *Darn it* under his breath, which made the class smile. But most importantly, he treated everyone equally. He didn't have favorites and he never made snide remarks to kids. He was just a regular guy who seemed to enjoy teaching and working with wood.

Mr. Middlefield scanned the seating chart for attendance and then typed into his computer any absent students. A moment later, he cleared his throat and adjusted his thin, circular glasses on his stubby nose. "New semester project, and it's big, folks. You'll have a full six weeks to plan and build the project. Seven if we need it." His thick fingers spread out in front of him and a smile curved his small mouth, nearly hidden within his beard. "I want you all to create something unique, and the more difficult, the higher the grade. Something out of the box. Use this project to stretch out of your comfort zone and expand on your creativity. But don't worry, I have a bunch of ideas to inspire you all laid out on my worktable here. I'll call you up by row and you can come and choose a project."

Sounds like fun, Travis thought.

When Travis's row was finally called, he stood behind the other kids. Even on his tiptoes he was too short to

ALONE TOGETHER

see over the others already crowded around the table; his growth spurt hadn't kicked in yet. When he finally squeezed his way to the front, Travis's mind leaped at the project ideas. There was a wood go-cart. Maybe he could get his dad to help him with the wiring, since it had wheels. He also spotted a mini lemonade stand and a pedaling wood horse.

But then he saw something different. It seemed to be a large cabinet with an automaton attached—a mechanical device shaped as a human figure—that could play a game of chess against an opponent. The chessboard was on top of the cabinet and the opponent could sit on the other side to play. In black marker, the picture was labeled underneath: MECHANICAL TURK.

Wow. Travis tilted his head in interest. Now, that idea looked challenging. He could pretty much lose himself in this project for a good while. But would it be *too* challenging? He still would like to get a good grade on the project. He looked around to see if there was something else that interested him, but his eyes kept veering back to the picture of the Mechanical Turk as if he was drawn toward it.

A kid named Pat whispered to someone next to him. "That Mechanical Turk looks tough. No way I'm choosing that one."

"Yeah, no way," the kid whispered back. "Looks like it could take way longer than six weeks to build."

Travis adjusted his hair as he studied the picture of the unique device. He *could* change the historical automaton that sat at a table to something else. Something more contemporary.

What about the sun from Freddy Fazbear's Mega Pizzaplex?

TALES FROM THE PIZZAPLEX

Technically he was thinking of Sun, an animatronic he'd seen on a commercial and on a poster outside the Pizzaplex building. He'd been intrigued by its bright yellow and red colors, and those bold sunrays that encircled his head. Travis had never liked the name Sun and had taken to calling him the Sunman in his mind. It's not like he had friends that would correct him. Adding the Sunman would really grab Mr. Middlefield's and the class's attention. Maybe he could even start making some friendships again. But it was okay if he *didn't* make any new friends, he quickly reasoned.

Travis envisioned the project as he walked back to his worktable. He saw the project in his mind and envisioned the pieces and the structure to bring it all together. He supposed that was what made him pretty good at woodshop class. He grabbed his notebook from his backpack and started sketching out the ideas he saw from the picture. He tapped his pencil on his chin. He would have to do some research on the inner workings of the device.

He smiled. This was going to be supercool.

Travis's dad had forgotten to pay his lunch tab at school again, even though he'd been reminding him. Not to mention, it had been tough for his dad to juggle things as a single father. Most of the time he forgot to do laundry or even run to the grocery store.

Travis spotted a couple of milks and a chocolate pudding on a table and grabbed the pudding. Some of the kids would leave food behind when they didn't want something. But who didn't want chocolate pudding? Travis slipped it into his backpack and continued out to the front of the school and sat under his favorite tree. He looked up at the long, gnarled branches that were dotted with yellow and orange leaves. They rustled in the slight cool breeze, but it was too early for them to fall.

He took out his notebook and opened to the page where he'd started sketching the Sunman. Since the Sunman was sitting behind the boxed cabinet, Travis wouldn't have to build the whole body, and so he focused on making detailed sketches of the automaton's arms and head.

As he was sketching, he felt a little tingle on the tip of his nose. He frowned. When it tingled again, he glanced up. Across from him, under another tree, was a girl he hadn't noticed before. She quickly looked down at her sketchbook as if she hadn't just been caught looking at him. She wore all black and had shoulder-length brown hair with streaks of purple.

Travis didn't know her name. He thought she might be new to Brighton Middle. Especially since she was sitting alone at lunch. He could go talk to her, he considered. Introduce himself and make a new friend.

But there was that funny pressure in the center of his chest at the idea so he didn't; instead, he continued working out the details of his project and pushed everything else out of his mind.

After school, Travis headed to the campus library. The hush of the huge room settled on him immediately. Students whispered. He heard pages turning and books sliding across shelves, and there was a musty scent that accompanied old books that had been handled for a long time. He used the library computer reserved for the catalog and was disappointed to find that there was only one book in the whole library about the Mechanical Turk.

Travis wrote down its location and scanned the rows of shelves. He wandered the shelves and then stopped short when the book wasn't there. He frowned and looked at his notecard, then looked back at the shelf. He was definitely in the right spot, but the book was apparently missing. He sighed. Someone must have checked it out already. Which meant someone else could be building the same project for woodshop class, too, or doing some sort of school report.

He shrugged. That was okay, he told himself. If it was for woodshop class, what was the chance they'd also be building the Sunman? Travis's project would still stand out. Probably.

He looked over at the librarian at the front desk. She had a line of kids she already had to help so he didn't bother waiting in line to ask for her assistance. It was better when he didn't have to talk to others anyway. He would just have to see what he could find on the computer on his own. He made his way over to the three computers in the library and they were already occupied by students.

He sighed again.

Maybe he could ask his dad if he'd ever heard of the Mechanical Turk before.

Maybe his dad could find some time to help Travis with a project this time.

Travis tried to visit his grandma before he got home. She lived a few blocks away in a small apartment complex for senior citizens. Grandma had called it home as long as Travis remembered. He walked down a row of doorways until he reached her apartment and knocked on the faded blue door.

ALONE TOGETHER

No one answered.

Travis shifted on his feet and knocked once more. She hadn't been home much recently, and he hoped she was okay. Maybe she was at a doctor's appointment or visiting a friend.

He was worried but mostly disappointed. Travis loved talking to her. Grandma always told him stories about growing up on her grandfather's farm, like how she'd been bucked from a horse or how she would chase the goats and chickens around their yard. She even told him old ghost stories and myths. He couldn't get enough of them.

He reached into his backpack and placed the chocolate pudding cup on the small doormat outside her door, hoping she'd come across it before a stray cat or dog snatched it. Chocolate pudding was Grandma's favorite; he always grabbed pudding cups for her when he could. Then he started off for home.

Travis had lived in the same neighborhood his whole life. It was a quiet street with large trees that were now shedding their autumn leaves onto the roads and gutters. A few of the sidewalks were cracked from the roots of the trunks. Families kept up their yards and occasionally there would be some construction work going on when someone replaced their roof or had their home refreshed with a new coat of paint. His dad hadn't done much to their house for a long time. The bushes tended to look overgrown, and there were always dead leaves on the tall grass. Occasionally, he did some yard work on the weekends and Travis would help him. When they were finished, they would sit in front of the TV for the rest of the quiet afternoon or Travis would go to his room to sketch new projects into his notebook.

Travis walked into the house and set his backpack on the floor. But then he remembered his mom used to not like that so he picked it back up. Their house had dark wood floors (he thought the stain was called Carrington), with matching baseboards. The walls were painted a pale blue, decorated with a few family photos and some bright pieces of artwork. Mom and Dad liked antiques and had spent years furnishing the house with secondhand furniture from estate sales and antique stores. It had been their thing to do together. Before.

A familiar blanket of sadness fell on Travis as he walked to his room.

There were a few posters on his walls. One was of Freddy Fazbear and some were of old cars that his dad always liked. Travis used to listen to his dad talk about vintage cars when he was little, and his dad had quizzed him on different years and makes of models for fun when they would spot one on the road. Travis smiled when a flash of memory came to him when he would go on drives with his dad in his vintage 1969 Nova. The car needed new paint, had taped-up black seats, with no interior on the roof or carpet on the floor, but Dad had rebuilt the engine and cut out the rusted parts on the body and rebuilt it all himself. Dad was super talented that way.

Those days were gone, though. There hadn't been any rides in the Nova for some time. Travis learned sadness was hard to overcome for him and his dad. He wished there was some kind of switch he could flick from melancholy to joy, but he was old enough to know that wasn't how life worked. Or that was what his grandma would tell him when he used to try to hold back tears if his feelings got hurt from kids teasing him because he was so shy.

ALONE TOGETHER

You got to feel your feelings, Trav. It's the only way to clear them out, but it takes time. There's no rushing about it.

Travis wasn't sure why, but as he stared at his room, he suddenly noticed it needed a good cleaning. His dresser and side table had a layer of dust across the top. His floor could use a vacuum, too. Dad didn't really do housework since he was at the shop for long days at a time. Travis would have to clean when he had a chance. He looked at his full backpack. But now he had a bunch of homework to do.

Mom used to joke that getting a conversation out of Dad was like pulling teeth. Mom was the chatty one, of course. She'd kept their home full of conversation, music, humming, jokes, and smiles. And now that she was gone and her sounds were all taken away, there was so much silence. Travis often thought of his home like a painting. When Mom was home, their life was like the colorful artwork she'd picked out for the walls, full of brightness and cheer. Now their home was like an outlined canvas, with only colors of gray and black.

That night, when Dad came home, Travis heard the front door open and shut. He walked out of his bedroom and watched his dad rifle through the mail. He tossed his keys onto the small table by the entry along with a few envelopes. He'd pulled off his dirty coveralls and left them at work, but his wrinkled T-shirt was still smeared with dark grease and dust. His hands were thick and strong, and the grease that he could never get completely clean was lined under his fingernails. His honey blond hair was sticking up in funny directions because he had a habit of running his hands through it when he was working out an issue with a car. His dirty boots were already off and left at the door.

"Hi, Dad," Travis called to him.

His dad sighed, ran a hand over the scruff on his hard jaw. For a moment, Travis thought he wouldn't answer, but then he finally said with a tired breath, "Hi, Trav."

They both stood there a moment in the silence of each other's company. His dad blinked a few times and then he went to take a shower. Travis went back to his homework.

Travis was sprawled out on his twin bed while he read his assigned reading. Some of his school notebooks were on his side table and a few books were on his bed. One thing he learned about middle school was that there was a lot more schoolwork. He didn't really mind, though, since it kept him pretty busy.

There was a knock at the door, and Dad walked into his room. Travis sat up on his bed, surprised. His dad usually met up with him in the kitchen for dinner.

Dad was freshly washed. Travis could smell the flowery shampoo. Dad had never changed the type of shampoo his mom always bought, even after she left. Dad wasn't good with change.

"Hey, Dad," Travis said.

His dad said hello with his usual meaningful glance and went straight to Travis's side table and picked up his woodshop notebook. He started to skim through the pages.

"Um," Travis began. "I have a new woodshop assignment. Those are my notes for an automaton device called a Mechanical Turk. I don't know if you've ever heard of

ALONE TOGETHER

it before. It's something from history." Travis lifted his cap and scratched at his head as his dad turned the pages.

His dad nodded. Then he smiled when he must have seen the sketch of the Sunman.

Travis's lips curved as he adjusted his hat back on. "I know I've never been inside the new Mega Pizzaplex, but sometimes when I walk by it I see the Sunman with the big smile on a poster, or when we watch those new commercials on TV. He's pretty cool looking with those sunrays around his head. Anyway, I know it's kind of silly. Um, I was wondering if maybe you could help me out with it?"

His dad scratched his jaw. "It's doable," he murmured. "You've always been creative, Trav."

Travis's eyes widened and his chest swelled up with pride. "Yeah? Thanks, dad. So you'll help me? I could really use the help. I don't know if I can finish it by myself within six weeks."

"Yep, it's doable," he said as he walked out of the room with the notebook in hand.

Travis followed behind him, excited as he expelled a relieved breath. "Maybe we could salvage some wood from your work yard and we wouldn't have to put too much money into it." Travis knew sometimes money was tight with a small family-owned business.

Dad placed Travis's notebook on the table and began to open two cans of chili and plopped the beans inside the pot on the stove. The kitchen was a good size and still had his mom's touches. The kitchen had deep white countertops and Mom would leave her favorite cooking devices out, such as her mixer and her coffee machine that steamed milk. Those were gone now but she'd left one of her favorite cookbooks and a couple of antique knickknacks. Travis wondered if she'd remember and come back and get them. He'd really like to see her. It had been a while.

Travis sat at the kitchen table, telling Dad about his day. He didn't mention how no one talked to him. He was embarrassed for his dad to know that he didn't have any friends.

"I went by grandma's again but she wasn't home. I think she might have had a doctor's appointment or something. And there's this new girl at school. She just sort of stared at me and then looked away when I saw her. I think she might not have any friends yet."

His dad grunted as he set two bowls of canned chili and slices of toasted bread on the table. It was one of their regular staples for dinner. Travis didn't mind. He liked chili.

They ate in silence as Travis watched his dad turn the pages of the notebook. Travis didn't have any more to say about school so he just watched his dad's expressions. He was just so glad his dad was ready to help with a school project again. He didn't want to say anything to change his mind.

When dinner was finished, Travis got up from his chair. "Well, I better go finish my homework. Thanks again for helping me with the Mechanical Sunman, Dad. It'll be fun, huh?"

His dad sat back in the chair, looked at Travis, and patted his own full belly. His mouth curved and he gave a little nod.

Travis smiled back, then jogged to his room and sat on his bed. He glanced at the picture on his side table. It

ALONE TOGETHER

was a picture of when Travis was little. Maybe he was in second grade. His mom and dad sat with him at a school picnic. They were each smiling. Travis remembered it had been such a fun day. They'd played games, had hot dogs, and the best part was they had been happy together.

Travis felt the familiar heavy feeling and his eyes began to burn. He blinked them away and went back to his school reading. There was nothing more to cry about; things were looking up because his dad was ready to help him again with the woodshop project.

It was going to be really great.

Travis scanned the computer search he typed in at the school library. He had to come in extra early in order to get a turn at the computer. When his dad left for work that morning, Travis awoke with the sound of the front door closing. He'd scrubbed at his tired face. He'd been dreaming of building the Mechanical Sunman, but the images faded away as soon as he woke.

On the computer's search engine, he eventually found a historical website dedicated to sharing information on his chosen woodshop project. The device had been seen as miraculous. In the eighteenth century, no one had ever played chess against an automaton before—it was way before AI and computer programming were commonplace. But it had all been an illusion.

Travis tapped his chin with his pencil. Why did he feel he knew this already? He guessed Mr. Middlefield had likely mentioned something to the class. There were hidden compartments built inside the cabinet where a person would hide and operate the automaton to play against the unknowing opponents.

Travis frowned at that. It sounded silly that no one knew the truth until many years later. An image flashed in Travis's mind of the cabinet's interior compartments, which were split into two hidden compartments covered by a faux wall, and he rubbed at his eyes. He hadn't slept well the night before, but he'd been pretty excited to have his dad on board with the project.

Travis sketched in his notebook as much as he could of the interior's hidden structure of the device, making a few notations on the dimensions that he could fit his entire body if he curled up his legs. For some reason, he had a flash of déjà vu as if he'd done this before. Researched. Sketched out the pictures. He shook his head. No, he knew he hadn't done any of this before . . .

The morning bell rang. Travis grabbed his notebook and backpack. He needed to stop by his locker for his history book. He walked out of the library and someone stepped in front of him and *actually* stopped.

Two black boots were lined up against his tennis shoes.

Travis was so surprised, he glanced up with wide eyes.

The new girl stood before him, and for a brief moment their gazes met.

She smells like cinnamon toast was his first thought.

Then, as he studied her face, he realized she had big, dark brown eyes with long lashes. Her nose was small and her lips were full.

Travis was caught so off guard, his mouth opened to say something. *Anything.* But all that came out was "Uhhhhhhh . . ."

The girl jerked her head down and detoured around him. Travis swallowed hard and watched her quickly walk away, not meeting anyone else's gaze. She wore an oversize black sweatshirt and black jeans. Her school bag, hanging from her shoulder, was mixed with purple and blue.

"*Uhhhhh?*" he repeated. He shook his head at his choice of vocabulary and hurried to his locker before the final bell rang. Next time, he'd have to introduce himself and ask her name.

Maybe.

Travis's mind drifted in class. He was back in woodshop, laying out tools on a worktable. He thought it was him because all he could see were hands building the structure. He was measuring the dimensions and cutting the slats of wood and then hammering the base of the cabinet together. Sure, Travis could envision how to make projects, but he had never before watched the perspective of his own hands building something as if he was watching from a distance—as if it was part of a movie. *Weird.*

The bell rang and Travis jerked back to the present.

"Tonight's assigned reading is on the board!" Mrs. Sullivan called out.

What?

Travis glanced down at his notebook and discovered that he hadn't take *any* notes.

Oh no. He looked around and watched everyone packing up for the next class. He hoped Mrs. Sullivan didn't have a pop quiz tomorrow on her lecture. What was going on with him?

Shaking his head, he stuffed his notebook and book into his backpack and headed out the door for second period.

* * *

When Travis walked up to his house after school, Dad's pickup truck was already in the driveway. He usually wouldn't be home for a few more hours. Travis's eyes widened as he rushed across the lawn to the front door.

Inside, he dropped his backpack and called out, "Dad? You home? Dad?"

There was no answer.

Travis rushed to the kitchen to find him, then to the living room. Even to his dad's bedroom, but he was nowhere to be found.

Huh.

Then he had a thought and rushed out to the backyard.

There was his dad, piling scraps of wood next to the work shed where he kept all his tools. The backyard was a small, square area, surrounded by a fence lined with overgrown ivy. The grass was usually dry and had patches of dirt because the yard had become the project area, where Travis and his dad liked to build things.

"Dad, you got the wood! That's great! We can get started right away!" Travis was beyond thrilled. Excitement rushed through him as he ran back inside the house and got his notebook out of his pack, then rushed back to his dad, telling him all the dimensions he gathered at the library as they got to work.

Travis was hammering at a piece of wood so hard that perspiration dampened his forehead. He stepped back and looked at the structure of the boxed cabinet he'd put together for the Mechanical Sunman. He ran his hand over the top of the wood and flinched back. *Ow.* He glanced at his hand to see a small drip of blood on the inside of his forefinger. He looked at the structure and spotted a sharp splinter of wood sticking out of the surface.

Suddenly, a fully built cabinet appeared before him . . . but the automaton was missing.

Travis stepped back in surprise. "Whoa . . ."

He spun around and noticed something else. He seemed to be surrounded by total darkness.

Bewildered, he said, "What's going on?" His voice echoed around him. He wasn't in his woodshop class. He wasn't at home. It was like a black abyss engulfed him. He looked down and saw there was no ground. Just darkness. He looked left, right, and above.

A chill of unease rippled down his back.

"Hello?!" he called out. "Where am I? Where is everyone?" Once again, his voice carried, echoing through the vastness. He began to walk through the bleak nothingness. "Dad? Mom?"

It felt like he had walked a long time when he finally heard footsteps and spotted a burst of light ahead of him. Travis picked up the pace to get to the light. He watched two forms moving in the distance. Or were they dancing?

As Travis made his way closer, he recognized the Sunman dancing in a circle. He was dressed in bright yellow, with accents of red. His nose was pointed and his smile was wide. His hands moved around, and Travis was very aware of his long, thin fingers. He wore puffy, striped pants and pointed shoes. When he moved, little bells jingled from his shoes and wrists. He was with another character . . . a brown bear, wearing a black bow tie and a tiny top hat that sat on his head. A blue lightning bolt was painted on his chest. Travis was pretty certain the bear was Glamrock Freddy from the Mega Pizzaplex. The bear went to sit at another boxed cabinet with a chessboard placed on the top. The playing pieces were red and yellow. The Sunman danced around the bear as he decided on his move on the chessboard.

Glamrock Freddy made a move with a red pawn. Then the animatronic got up from the table to walk around, swaying to the music, but when he'd rose, the bear knocked over a couple of board pieces. The Sunman rushed over to set the fallen pieces right again on the board, then he took a seat on the other side of the table and stared at the board as he moved his head to the music.

Travis wasn't sure what to do. He was mesmerized by them. He felt like he was in another world, as if he'd been slipped into a movie or video game. Should he try to speak to them?

The Sunman made his move with a yellow pawn and then got up to dance around Travis, encircling him and waving his arms to the music, which seemed to be speeding up. As the beats of the music played faster, the Sunman danced more erratically.

"Um, hello." Travis turned with him, trying to follow him, but he started to get dizzy. "Stop," Travis told him, holding up his hands. "Please. I don't understand what's happening. Please slow down. Where am I? Why am I here?"

Suddenly, the music stopped and so did the Sunman—right in front of Travis, leaning down toward Travis's face. Too close. Travis sucked in a breath as the Sunman's round, pale white eyes stared intently into his. Travis trembled from his odd intensity.

"Why does it all seem so familiar?" the Sunman whispered gleefully.

Travis woke up in his bed, breathing hard. His hand shook as he ran it over his face.

He licked his dry lips and murmured, "*Why* does it all seem so familiar?"

All day through school, Travis had this strange, nagging feeling. It was that feeling like he'd forgotten an important assignment at home that was due. Travis checked his backpack and was sure he had all his assignments, and he didn't really have anything else to do but go to school. It was like something was off but he just couldn't put his finger on it. He hardly paid attention in his classes, and instead stared at his notes for his woodshop project. He studied the Sunman sketch and kept replaying the strange dream in his mind.

Should he talk to his dad about this odd, familiar feeling he'd been having? Or would that just distract his dad from helping him with the project? He hoped his grandma was home after school. She was always good with helping him try to figure things out.

Luckily, he found an extra chocolate pudding left out at lunch and he stuck it in his backpack for later. He walked to the front of the school to go sit under his tree and discovered it was occupied!

By the new girl.

She was sitting in *his* usual spot under the tree, sketching in her book.

Travis blew out an annoyed breath. He glanced at the tree he'd noticed her under before and observed that there were two other kids sitting under it. She'd been kicked out of her spot, too.

He almost turned around and walked away. He had too much on his mind. Maybe he could go to the library?

Then he took a breath and decided on a whim to walk over to the girl. He felt his breathing increase and his jaw clench as he made his way closer.

He stopped in front of her and adjusted his backpack. His stomach felt like it was twisted in knots. He opened his mouth and nothing came out. He swallowed hard.

"H-hey," he finally managed.

Her shoulders stiffened and she dropped her head lower into her book. Her hand seemed to clench around her pencil even tighter.

"Um, this is, uh, my usual spot," he told her.

She mumbled something.

Travis lifted his eyebrows. "What?"

"I said, I don't see your name on it," she spoke quietly, without looking up at him.

"Oh. No, but I sit here every day. It's my usual spot for lunch. Since you're new, you probably didn't know that and it's okay. Really."

"Well, I'm here now. So. Go. Away."

Travis frowned. She wasn't very friendly and she wasn't going to give up the tree. He looked on the other side of the trunk. "Mind if I sit on the other side?"

"Fine. Just stop talking to me," she hissed.

Travis shook his head. *Sheesh.* She wasn't nice at all. "All right. Fine." He walked around the tree and dumped his backpack on the ground and sat with his back to her. He took out his notebook to make a list of the materials he was going to need for the Mechanical Sunman.

ALONE TOGETHER

Gosh. He'd rather she'd just ignore him than talk mean to him.

After school, Travis eagerly took off to his grandma's apartment. He had so much to talk about with her. He knocked on her apartment door, not really expecting her to be home—but hoping—when he heard her call out, "Come in!"

Grandma was finally home!

Relieved, Travis walked into her studio apartment, smelling the vanilla-scented candle she would usually light. He spotted her right away sitting in her brown recliner in front of her television. She was watching a game show where families compete against each other to solve guessing games on funny topics. But he noticed a few things were different. She seemed to have gotten a new couch and a coffee table. There was even a new tablecloth on her little table, covered with purple plums.

"Travis! It's so good to see you!" Grandma had curly gray hair and a smile that was always friendly. She never wore glasses, even though she had a hard time reading small print. Grandma was stubborn that way. She liked to wear colorful tops. Today's was full of pretty, bright flowers.

"Grandma, I've been coming over but you haven't been home."

She waved a hand in the air. "Oh, just visiting old friends. Doing some traveling. I've been on some new adventures, Trav! I visited so many great places. I'm going on another trip soon. I can't wait!"

"Wow, really? Another trip?" Travis felt a little disappointed she was leaving again. When he was able to visit with her, he didn't feel so lonely, even if it was for a short time.

"I have some new stories to tell you after we catch up!"

"Can't wait to hear about them." Travis smiled. He pulled out the pudding from his backpack and retrieved a spoon from the kitchenette for her.

Grandma's eyes widened as he handed them over, and she smiled with joy. "Looks good, Trav, thank you. So what have you been up to? How's your dad?" She dug into her pudding.

Travis sat in a wood chair by her small table. "I've just been going to school. Dad is . . . good. He's going to help me with a school project."

Her eyebrows lifted in surprise. "Hmm. Really?"

Travis nodded.

She studied him a moment, then asked, "Make any new friends lately?"

"No, not really." Travis shook his head, then he thought about the new girl. Grandma knew he was shy. She was always telling him to go out and meet new kids. Well, he'd tried speaking to one today and she had been mean. "Well, there's this new student, a girl, but she doesn't talk to anybody and when I did talk to her, she didn't even look at me. She wasn't very friendly. At all."

"Maybe she's shy like you, Trav."

Travis thought that over. "I don't know . . ." He hadn't seen her talking to anyone else.

"Go ahead and try to talk to her again. Maybe the next time won't be so bad."

He tilted his head, considering. "Maybe. I'll think

ALONE TOGETHER

about it. I wanted to run something by you, Grandma. Something weird that's been going on."

Her eyebrows lifted and her smile bloomed. "Oooh, sounds like a good beginning to a story," she told him. "Tell me all about it. I got plenty of time."

He adjusted his ball cap and proceeded to tell her about his woodshop project and the details of the Mechanical Sunman. How, as he researched the details, strange images had been flashing in his mind. Things had seemed really familiar, as if he'd experienced it all before. But he knew they weren't his memories.

"I mean," he continued, "I've never even heard of the automaton device before, so these can't be my thoughts. But why would I keep remembering researching and building the cabinet before when I haven't? I just don't understand what's going on."

Grandma licked her lips as she finished her chocolate pudding. "Hmm. Could be, you might have a ghost on your hands."

Travis's eyes widened. "A ghost?"

She nodded. "Oh yeah. I was haunted by a ghost once."

"How did you know you were haunted?"

"Well, there's five signs a ghost is around you."

Travis leaned forward, intrigued. "Really? What are the signs, Grandma?"

Grandma held up a forefinger. "One: You start to have funny dreams and flashes of memories that are not yours. It's like they possess your thoughts when they're near."

She flashed two fingers and so forth, counting the signs. "Two: You can feel chills or a tingle on your arms or back when they're around.

"Three: There could be sudden movements of objects or sounds out of the blue.

"Four: If they really attach themselves to you, sometimes you can hear thoughts in your head as if the ghost is talking to you.

"Five: And if you are really gifted, and this is pretty rare, you might even see the ghost with your own eyes."

Travis sat back in his chair with his mouth gaping in surprise. "*Wow*. That's amazing." Some of those signs sounded exactly like what was going on with Travis. Definitely one and two. A chill radiated down his back at the thought of a ghost possessing his thoughts. "So I may be sensitive to this ghost?" *So unreal.* "Who was your ghost, Grandma?"

"A woman who had died years ago on my daddy's land. Most ghosts linger around the place they died, especially if their remains are undiscovered. They travel around the places that are familiar to them."

"What did you do about her?"

She shook her head with a long sigh. "There was nothing I could do. I didn't know how to help yet. I would have vivid dreams about her old life on the farm. I tried to tell my ma and daddy, but they didn't believe me. For weeks, I searched high and low on every inch of the land. Couldn't find her body, though. So I had to just live with her around every so often till I grew up and moved away. She wasn't so bad after a while. I got used to her."

Travis couldn't imagine having these weird feelings and images all through middle school, distracting him from his schoolwork and projects. "Since this has to do with my current school project, do you think it's an older student of Brighton Middle School? Someone who had been at the school some time ago?"

She nodded. "Could be."

"But why now? Why me?"

"Could be there's a familiar tie between the two of you with the same project you're set to build. Anything special about this cabinet?"

"Well, it's pretty unique. It has hidden cabinets inside that can be kind of tricky."

"A ghost that's haunting you about a project with hidden cabinets. Hmm."

Travis frowned. "You don't think the ghost's body is trapped inside the cabinet? But that would mean . . ."

Grandma scooted forward in her recliner, her eyes eager with excitement, but there was something else in her eyes as if she knew something that he didn't. It was hard to tell with Grandma.

"Yep, if it is a ghost," she told him, "your ghost may have died at your school, Trav! He might need you to help find him so he can move on. He could be trapped in that thingamajig, waiting to be discovered. Wouldn't that be something?"

Travis swallowed hard. "Yeah. That'd be something." It was really a lot to take in, especially now that he had his hands full building the woodshop project with his dad. "Well, um, I better get going. I hope you have a good trip, Grandma. I'll miss you."

His grandma smiled at him. She opened her arms and Travis stood to give her a hug. He felt a brief comfort as she patted his back. "I'll tell you about my new adventures another time. You'll find your answers, Trav, just like I did. Don't you worry."

TALES FROM THE PIZZAPLEX

★ ★ ★

Travis walked into his house and looked out the window at the backyard and the structure of the Mechanical Sunman he and his dad had started to put together. It was bare boned at the moment, with no sides—just some pieces of wood to form the main box of the cabinet. A sudden feeling of panic rushed over him. He flashed to darkness and heavy breathing as if someone had been inside something dark. His hands went out in front of him as if he was shut inside something wooden. Travis's chest tightened, and he grew so hot he actually began to sweat. He thought about what his grandma had said . . .

He might need you to help find him so he can move on. He could be trapped in that thingamajig, waiting to be discovered.

Travis fisted his hands together, trying to pull himself out of the ghost's feelings. "It's not my memory. *It's not my memory.*" He took in a big breath and exhaled as the memory drifted away. "This is what I have to do," he murmured. "I have to find the ghost's body." Travis looked again at the beginnings of the woodshop project. "Sorry, Dad, I'm going to need to take a little break on the project to help someone out. I hope you understand."

If a student had died inside the cabinet at school, maybe Mr. Middlefield still had the structure in storage. Travis couldn't investigate stuff when everybody was there, though. He needed to be able to get into the past school files without being seen, in order to find out more information about a missing student.

He rushed to his room and scribbled a note on a piece of paper to his dad that he was staying the night at his friend Pete's house. Not that he'd spoken to Pete in a long time, but his dad wouldn't really know that. Then

ALONE TOGETHER

he grabbed a clean set of clothes and stuffed them in his backpack with his books and notebooks and rushed to the kitchen to grab an apple and banana. He ran out the house and took off back to the school before Mr. Hadley, the janitor, locked it up for the night.

Travis jogged all the way to the school. He had to admit that being haunted was pretty interesting. Travis lived a pretty uninteresting life. He went to school, he went home, and he did his homework on repeat. Now with the ghost entering his life, it was like he was feeling emotions he hadn't felt in some time. Eagerness. Anticipation. Interest.

When he got to the front steps of the school, he was breathing hard and perspiring on his face. He scanned to see if anyone was around. He spotted a couple of kids sitting outside, but they weren't paying attention to him, so he slipped through the main doors. The hallways were quiet except for a few murmurs from teachers still in their classrooms. Travis couldn't help noticing how odd it felt being in school when it was nearly empty. He wracked his brain on where to hide for the time being. He settled on the library, where he could use the librarian's computer to access the school's network.

Travis looked up at the ceiling for the school's security cameras, which were attached to certain areas of the hallways. He had never really paid attention to them before. But now he realized that he could be caught sneaking around on camera and get in big trouble. Luckily, there weren't a lot of cameras, and they were often pointed in one direction. He might be able to avoid some of the cameras by pressing himself against the walls and out of view. Just not all of them.

He tiptoed by the bathrooms and then quickly walked down the hallway, trying to appear normal. If he ran into someone, he'd just say, *Oh, I forgot a book I needed for my homework.* Not that he was good at fibbing. His mom had always known he was fibbing because his cheeks would grow red.

He was about to turn a corner when he heard two teachers chatting and walking closer. Travis glued himself against the lockers and held his breath as they walked by, not noticing him.

Whew. That was close.

After the teachers passed, he rushed to the library door. There was a camera above the entryway. If he glued himself to the other side of the hallway, he might not be filmed. Travis pressed himself against the wall and snuck under the camera's view. Luckily, the door was still unlocked. He walked quietly into the library. He heard the copy machine working in the back room behind the counter, so Travis rushed to the farthest bookshelves and crouched down and hid in a corner.

With his heart beating fast in his chest, he hunkered down to wait until the librarian left for the evening. He hoped she didn't stay too long.

About an hour later, after he heard the librarian leave and lock the door, Travis crept over to her computer. His stomach felt twisted with nerves. The lights were off and the daylight had drifted away to evening through the windows. He hoped his dad found his note and wasn't worried about him. As Travis looked around, he tried to shake off an uneasy feeling that he was doing something wrong.

ALONE TOGETHER

"I'm not hurting anyone. I'm just trying to help out a ghost," he told himself. Honestly, that just made him feel weirder.

He couldn't help thinking that the ghost was just a lonely kid like him, trying to find his way. Every day felt like that to Travis. He wasn't really good with change. He hadn't adjusted to not having both his parents together. He still wore his Little League hat, even though he had only played a couple of seasons. He'd often struck out and kids made fun of him when he couldn't catch a fly ball. His dad had been a little disappointed when he had quit since he liked to help the coach out and spend time with him doing something fun. Travis wore the hat to remind them of the times they'd spent together, even if it hadn't been perfect.

Now Travis realized he should have kept playing Little League for his dad. He should have ignored the teasing kids so he could be closer with him. Maybe instead of all the quiet evenings, it would have forced his dad to talk and interact more with Travis. A little too late now.

The computer stopped rebooting and flashed with a password request on the screen.

Oh no. Travis rubbed at his face. *Now what?*

Maybe the librarian had the password written down somewhere. He started looking around the desk for a note. He saw a few papers taped around the computer but nothing that looked like a password. Then he opened a top drawer in her desk. He found a couple mint candies. Pens and pencils. Paper clips. A key ring with a few keys. He spotted a leather-bound notebook and grabbed it. Sure enough, in the inside top corner was written:

Password—Library1234!

Travis quickly typed it into the password box, and he was logged into the school system. *Yes!*

He put the notebook back and shut the drawer, then clicked into the school's system with the computer mouse, trying to figure out where to go next.

"Hmm, where to?"

There were tons of folders and a whole network of school information that he wasn't familiar with. He tapped his chin. He guessed he should look for records of any missing students.

In the search feature, he typed in: *Missing Students.*

Nothing showed up.

"Okay, how about here." He began to look through a ton of folders on the past students of Brighton Middle, but none of them noted that any students had disappeared. Although there were time periods of when students attended the school. He sighed. How could he think it would so easy? But he knew the ghost had to have been in woodshop class, since he had likely built the same automaton device that Travis chose to build.

He looked into Mr. Middlefield's class rosters, but the lists of names didn't help since he didn't know the ghost's name yet. And there was nothing that notated grades or special projects. Mr. Middlefield likely kept that information in his own files. Travis considered going to woodshop class next. But he wasn't sure he could avoid the camera that was inside the large classroom. Travis recalled seeing the camera pointed directly toward the center of the room, straight at Mr. Middlefield's computer.

He then searched through some of the technical folders, and he came across the CCTV network, which was the closed-circuit cameras for the school's security system. He started scanning the camera footage for the previous years in the woodshop class. It seemed the school had upgraded just recently. There was an older system that only saved camera shots a few times a day and stored the snapshots in dated folders. There were hundreds and hundreds of files, Travis realized.

This could take forever!

Well, he was already this far, and he was determined to help the ghost.

Travis took out his apple from his backpack and started eating it as he settled in for the evening to scan all the footage from previous woodshop classes.

Hours passed. Travis's eyes drooped; he straightened in the chair and blinked his eyes rapidly in order to stay alert. "Come on, stay awake. Focus."

When he zeroed in on the screen, he realized he finally found something.

It was a picture of the woodshop class filled with projects. However, the picture must have been taken after school because there weren't any students in the classroom. The worktables were empty and there were projects gathered together in a corner section of the class that the students must have been working on.

Sure enough, Travis finally discovered evidence of a mechanical chess-playing device sitting on a cabinet, but this one was with an unfinished automaton, with spikes around the head.

Spikes?

Like sunrays?

Travis gasped. *It was really true.* He was being haunted by a ghost from Brighton Middle School. The dreams, the memories Travis had been having, were all from the kid who had built the device before him and had somehow died.

They both wanted to build the same project with the Sunman theme and that was likely why the ghost was drawn to Travis, flooding him with his memories and feelings.

Had Travis even wanted to build the Sunman, or was it all the ghost's influence?

The ghost was calling out to Travis to help him. To find him.

Somewhere on the school grounds.

Possibly from inside the hidden compartments of the Mechanical Sunman cabinet!

Travis shoved out of the chair and began to pace in front of the librarian's computer. He whipped off his hat and ran his hand through his hair. He couldn't believe this was really happening. Grandma was right. The ghost had chosen Travis to help him because of the connection to the same project.

Am I even up to such a task? he wondered. He was just a seventh grade loner. He didn't think his dad would even believe him if he told him about his suspicions.

But the ghost was all alone with no one to help him.

Just waiting to be found. To be seen.

A sensation hitched in Travis's gut. He knew what it felt like to be unseen. He knew what it was like to feel all alone.

Travis took a big breath. He had to help him.

He had to find the ghost's body so he wouldn't be alone anymore.

Determined, Travis flipped his hat on his head and sat back at the computer. The photo had been taken over two years ago. He searched through the next few snapshots to see when the automaton device disappeared from the woodshop class. The next group of pictures showed the woodshop projects slowly disappearing from the classroom. Two weeks later, a couple school workers were pictured carrying out the unfinished Mechanical Sunman.

"There you are," he murmured. "But where did they take you?"

It had to be somewhere on the school grounds.

Travis tried to search for other snapshots in the hallways to see if he could get an idea of the direction the school workers were headed, but he couldn't find anything else.

He sat back in the chair, a little defeated.

He wracked his brain on what to do next, then his eyes widened when another idea hit. He needed a map of the entire school grounds in order to find all the storage facilities.

Travis decided to search for a map of the school. He would search each and every one of the storage areas until the Mechanical Sunman was discovered and the lonely ghost's body was found.

The next morning, Travis was exhausted. He'd been up all night. After he found a map of the entire school grounds, he printed out sections of the map with the librarian's printer, then took the time to shut everything back down, leaving no evidence of his visit behind. He waited, crouched in his hiding place until the librarian came in for the day and went into her back room, and then Travis rushed out before she could see him. He'd changed his clothes in the boy's bathroom and went to his regular classes in a cloudy haze. In first period history class, Mrs. Sullivan liked to jack up the heater. With the warmth, Travis nearly drifted asleep. Wouldn't that have been embarrassing if Mrs. Sullivan had called on him and everyone laughed at him for taking a nap!

At lunch, he went to his usual spot under the tree. Luckily, the new girl wasn't there. He pulled out pages of the map and started circling all the storage areas on the school grounds.

There were seven school storage areas throughout the map: a gym storage area, an attic above the school office, the basement, two sheds by the track, a closet in the art department, and the janitor's workroom.

This was going to take a while.

He knew Mr. Hadley was walking around the lunch area at this time. He could sneak over to his workroom and take a quick look before lunch ended.

Suddenly energized, Travis hopped up and jogged over to the workroom, his pack knocking onto his back. When he got to the door, he looked around to see if the coast was clear.

With his hand behind him, he wiggled the knob and discovered the door was unlocked!

Attempting to do a little nonchalant whistle, he quickly ducked into the workroom and closed the door behind him. His pulse was fluttering. He hoped he didn't get caught.

It was a pretty large room with two lights on. One was near the doorway and the other was near the back over a worktable. Travis walked through the room, scanning around. The room was jammed with shelves that were lined with cleaning supplies and tools. There were brooms, mops, shovels, and a couple of rakes. A shelf was filled with paint cans and rollers. There were tools stuffed on one shelf, with small boxes of nails and screws. There were broken desks shoved against one wall and a couple of school flags folded on a shelf. A mini fridge was set on a small table near the back worktable, and a few thank-you cards were taped to the wall for Mr. Hadley.

There was no wood automaton device to be found.

The eagerness he felt when he rushed over to the workroom deflated like a flat balloon.

"Not here," he muttered as he took out his maps and a pencil and checked off the janitor's workroom. "It's okay. There's a lot more places you could be." Then he left out the way he came. He turned the corner of the small building, and there was the new girl, sitting alone against the wall of the workroom, sketching in her notebook.

Travis halted abruptly. He remembered the unwelcoming conversation he'd had before and was ready to turn right around. But he also remembered his grandma encouraging him to try to talk with her again, because she could be shy like him.

Come on, come on. Take a step.

He forced his legs to move toward her and slowly walked closer. Before he reached her, he had a handful of reasons he should leave her alone.

She didn't like him.

She was shy and wanted to be left alone.

She wasn't friendly at all.

She probably thought he was a complete dork.

He cleared his throat anyway and wiped his damp palms down the front of his shirt.

Her head whipped up as she looked at him, then around them. Travis scanned about, too. Kids didn't really venture over to this area of the school at lunch.

"I'm not under your tree," she muttered to him, getting back to her sketching.

Travis lifted his eyebrows when he glimpsed her sketching a graveyard with skulls and bones. Maybe she'd be interested in hearing about his ghostly experience.

"Oh, I know. Um, thanks for that. I had to do something over here. Um, my name's Travis. What's yours?"

She let out an annoyed sigh. "Marissa."

"So you're new here, huh?"

She nodded.

"Mind if I sit with you?"

She shrugged. "Fine, whatever. It's a free country."

Relieved, Travis sat next to her but not too close. "So, where are you from?"

"Manor Hall Middle."

Travis recalled it was the middle school on the other side of town.

"So you must have moved with your family?"

She blew out a breath as if she was annoyed with his questions. "Why are you even here? What do you want?"

Travis blinked, surprised by her direct questions. "Um, just making friends."

"Well, I don't want to be friends, okay?"

Travis didn't say anything for a moment. Then he figured he could answer one of her questions. "Well, I'm actually here trying to help out a ghost."

She whipped her head toward him, but when they met gazes, she quickly looked away. "What do you mean?"

ALONE TOGETHER

Pleased she was interested, he settled in to explain what he'd been experiencing. "Well, I've been getting these feelings and memories from a ghost that I think died somewhere here on the school grounds. He could be trapped within a wood cabinet. I call it the Mechanical Sunman." He went on to explain the woodshop project and its historical origins. "I'm trying to find him so I can help him. I think when I find his body, he'll be able to move on."

Marissa's hand froze on the pencil she was using to draw.

Travis's face heated. Why had he said this?

"Pretty weird, I know." He swallowed nervously and rolled his shoulders, trying to ease the tension there.

She finally started drawing in her sketchbook again. She didn't say anything for a few moments, and then said, "Interesting."

A feeling of relief washed over him. Maybe he was finally making a new friend.

"So . . . where are you looking?" she actually asked. "For this ghost?"

Smiling, Travis showed her the printouts of the maps, pointing out all the places he intended to search. She would occasionally glance over to the pages of the map, then to her sketchbook, and back again.

"I just checked out the janitor's workroom. Nothing there. I have all these other places to search." He tapped his feet on the concrete ground. "Um, so, do you want to help me?" he asked, gripping tightly to the papers. "I bet with two of us, we can find the cabinet and the ghost's body even faster."

She shook her head and grimaced. "No way do I want to find a dead body."

Travis's hopes sunk. Yeah, he guessed it would be kind of gross. He didn't really think about what it would be like to find the ghost's dead body. He'd been so focused on finding the Mechanical Sunman that it hadn't crossed his mind that he'd actually find a corpse.

Jeez, he really was a dork sometimes.

The warning bell signaled that lunch was over.

Marissa gathered up her stuff and they both stood. Marissa stepped around him and started walking away.

Travis swallowed hard. *Just do it. Just ask!* "Um, Marissa, maybe we could hang out at the Pizzaplex together after school one day . . . it looks really—"

She whirled around with wide eyes. "*No!* I don't want to hang out with you. All right?"

Travis flinched. He swallowed hard from the rejection and he felt his shoulders sag.

A little hitch clenched in his gut.

He looked down at the ground as he shifted his feet. "Oh, okay. Sure. I understand. No problem. Maybe, we could just talk again sometime . . . by ourselves?" Travis asked her hesitantly. "We don't have to *go* anywhere together." He peeked up at her under the brim of his hat.

She seemed to eye him suspiciously. "I don't know. *Maybe.*" Then she rushed away from him.

A little light of hope sparked inside him. Maybe Marissa would decide to be his friend after all . . . eventually.

Before he knew it, the final bell rang after lunch. A few kids started rushing to classes. He was late, too.

Then he thought of the ghost.

Forgotten and hidden away.

ALONE TOGETHER

He had to continue his search of the school's storage facilities.

Travis wasn't sure how long he searched that afternoon but he knew it was a long time. He'd snuck around the school grounds during the last two classes, in order to avoid any campus supervisors, and then continued his search after school ended. He went through the art department's storage room, checking behind costumes and big theater displays. He scoured through painted canvases and jugs of paint and glue. He pulled out heavy boxes and moved around old furniture. Tired and sweaty, he sat on the floor after realizing the Mechanical Sunman wasn't there, either.

Art department: check.

After that he headed to the gym's storage area, which was close by in the school auditorium. He found the door unlocked and he shuffled through old jerseys and boxes of deflated basketballs. He found some plastic activity cones, Hula-Hoops, and extra chairs and tables. A pile of activity binders were stacked on the floor. A loudspeaker and microphone were stored in there for the principal to speak to students when they gathered for assemblies. But still there was no sign of the unfinished automaton device. So he marked the two storage areas off his list and thought he'd better head home to see his dad. He could be wondering where he was by now.

He rushed to get home as the day had already darkened to evening and a cold wind was blowing leaves across his path. But when he got home, his dad's truck wasn't in the driveway and the house was still dark.

Travis walked into the living room and checked to

see if his dad had made any progress on his woodshop project.

Somehow, the Mechanical Sunman was halfway complete!

He stopped in front of it, studying the structure. The boxed cabinet was completely put together. The doors had yet to be put on and it wasn't yet sanded and stained. The Sunman had yet to be built. There was a chunk of wood sitting at the table, waiting to be carved and painted.

"Amazing," he said in awe. "Dad, how did you manage to make so much progress so quickly?" Dad must have been working on it all night long, he realized.

Travis had a twinge of guilt that he hadn't been there to help him. He was torn between helping the ghost and spending time with his dad, when Travis had asked for his dad's help on the project in the first place.

But the thing was, Travis had also been asked for help and he was doing his best to fulfill the request.

That evening after Dad finally got home, they had dad's favorite dinner of chili and a slice of toasted bread. Travis was distracted and his dad seemed to be, too. They barely talked. Travis wanted to thank him for all the work he'd done on the Mechanical Sunman but since Dad wasn't saying much, he didn't, either.

He must be upset with him, Travis realized. When his dad was disappointed, he sometimes gave Travis the silent treatment until he wasn't that upset anymore.

Travis felt guilty for upsetting his dad. But he just wanted to find the ghost's body and he couldn't do it until the morning when he went back to school.

ALONE TOGETHER

Travis had his elbow propped on the table and leaned his head in his hand, staring at his chili beans. When his dad shoved away from the table, he started to clean up the bowls. Travis got up from his chair.

"I have some homework to finish. So good night, Dad," he said, and walked to his room.

"'Night, Trav," his dad murmured, clearly distracted.

Travis was so tired from the last couple of days, he fell into his bed and dropped off into oblivion.

Travis woke up in bed to a murmuring voice. He blinked, trying to understand who was talking.

It was his dad. But who was he talking to?

Travis sat up and rubbed the sleepiness from his eyes. It sounded like his dad was talking on the phone to someone.

Travis rose from his bed and walked into the hallway, trying to figure out who he was talking to, but his dad spoke so quietly that he couldn't catch much of what he was saying.

". . . sometimes . . . Travis . . ."

He was talking about Travis. Maybe he was talking to Travis's mom!

"I even . . . a habit . . . I know, I know."

Travis quietly tiptoed back into his bedroom to get ready for school. As Travis got dressed, he heard his dad leave for work. Travis wondered why they were talking about him. Was it because Travis skipped some classes yesterday and they found out? Was Dad telling Mom how he was disappointed that Travis wasn't putting the work into the school project?

TALES FROM THE PIZZAPLEX

He *shouldn't* be skipping class. He *should* be helping more with the project. He didn't want to upset his dad or his mom. It's just that everything inside him told him to find the ghost's body. So if he had to miss a few classes, so be it.

Once he found the body, it would be all over the school and his dad would have to understand why he was so distracted.

Sheesh. It wasn't easy being haunted!

Since he got to school early and there weren't that many kids or teachers there yet, Travis felt it was a good time to see if he could get into the school basement. He strolled over to a door that had a sign posted:

BASEMENT

FACULTY ONLY

NO STUDENTS ALLOWED

Travis tapped his chin with a finger.

Should he be breaking any more school rules?

Probably not. Then he threw his hands up.

Why stop now? He was, after all, on a very important mission.

He checked for the direction of the security camera and was relieved that it was pointed toward the hallway in the opposite direction of the basement. Travis pushed through the door. A creepy, cemented stairway led down into darkness. He took a breath, stepped in, and shut the door at his back. Travis blinked a few times trying to adjust his eyes to the dark. He looked around for a light switch but he didn't see one.

He felt the wall with his open palm as he slowly walked down each step, trying to feel for a switch. Since he stepped down slowly in order not to fall, it took some time to get to the bottom of the stairs. He finally felt a switch and flicked on the light.

A single light dangled on a long cord from the ceiling.

Brighton Middle School must have been around for a long time because the basement appeared really old and dingy. It smelled of rat droppings and stinky mold. The walls were covered with a cracked tile. There were boxes of old books on metal shelves that were shoved against walls, along with a few antique-looking desks. A few rolled-up posters and maps were stacked in a box in one corner.

An ancient furnace was on one wall and on the opposite was some kind of switchboard that he guessed powered the school's electricity. He walked around the basement area, turning corners into a couple of rooms. But the other rooms didn't seem to have any working lights. As his eyes scanned the darkness, he looked around for large objects that could be shaped like a cabinet but couldn't find anything similar. Travis was pretty sure the rooms were just filled with more outdated school books. He spotted the shapes of a couple of office desks and a few office chairs. Travis turned around and walked back to the center of the basement, searching for the Mechanical Sunman but, of course, it wasn't there, either.

"When am I going to find it?" he wondered aloud.

Was it even still on the school grounds?

It had to be since the ghost was haunting around the school, right? But there seemed to be so many ghost rules.

He was just going by what Grandma had told him, and he wasn't sure she was an actual expert on the subject.

How did people come up with these ghost rules, anyway? Considering the ghosts were dead and not easy to talk to.

Suddenly, his chest began to grow tight and he pressed a hand there. His breathing thinned and he started to panic.

Oh no, not again.

The ghost was overpowering Travis with its feelings once more!

Travis tried to suck in gulps of air.

The light bulb burst above him, engulfing him in complete darkness.

Scared, Travis spun around, reaching his hands out, attempting to feel his way toward the stairs to get out.

He couldn't see anything! He couldn't breathe! He needed help!

He stumbled forward and tripped on something, falling forward. He knocked his knees hard on the stairs. Pain radiated up his shins.

The stairway out!

He climbed up on his hands and knees. When he got to the door, he stood and pushed it open and rushed out, with his heart pounding fast in his chest.

He charged into the middle of the hallway. Kids flooded the floor, getting ready to go to class. He spun around bewildered, adjusting to the bright sunlight peering through the front doors. Some kids brushed past him. Others just looked at him.

He wanted to yell, *A ghost is haunting me! Someone, help me out here!*

ALONE TOGETHER

But he couldn't.

No one would believe him.

No one would likely care.

He spotted Marissa walking down the hallway. He stepped toward her to tell her what he just experienced. He needed to tell someone.

"*Marissa,*" he called to her.

But something was different about her. Her head wasn't tilted down at the floor. Her eyes were cheerful and she stood up straight. Her cheeks looked to have a little pink on them. She was actually smiling.

At him?

He smiled back and walked toward her, ready to tell her everything that just happened. Then he noticed her walking with a new friend, a girl who Travis believed was named Trish. They were talking and smiling at each other.

He waited for Marissa to say hi. To just look at him or acknowledge him in some way.

But she just continued to walk by him without a glance, without a word.

"Marissa?" He called again as she walked by him, but she completely ignored him as if he didn't exist to her. As if she'd never even spoken to him before.

His heart seemed to squeeze in his chest.

Marissa didn't want to be his friend.

He wasn't good enough for her.

He wasn't good enough for anybody.

What was so wrong with him?

Why was he such a loner? A nobody that no one cared about?

Not even his parents.

TALES FROM THE PIZZAPLEX

Maybe if he had just cleaned his room more. Or told his mom he loved her more often. Maybe she'd left because he'd been too much trouble to take care of. His mom was always cooking for him, cleaning up after him, making sure he was doing his homework. His parents had begun to fight as if out of nowhere. He would get so upset listening to them that he would rush to his room and slam the door until they finally stopped and realized he was witnessing it all.

He felt tears well up and wiped them away with the back of his hand. He couldn't cry in front of the other kids. They'd never let him live it down.

The pit in his stomach seemed to grow bigger as he started to walk. The final bell rang to go to class, but he didn't want to go. What was the use? He never spoke to anyone. He never did any of the fun things the other kids did.

Maybe it was his destiny to be alone forever.

So Travis did something he'd never done before.

He walked out the front doors, off the lawn of the school grounds, and he ditched school.

Travis walked around town for the rest of the day. The sky was a dismal gray with low-hanging clouds. He walked to the Mega Pizzaplex, staring at the neon lights that flashed across the big sign. The parking lot was filled with cars even on a weekday. He looked at the animatronic pictures on the windows, staring at Glamrock Freddy and Montgomery Gator, waving with their hands as if to invite customers in. Travis thought about going in, but he didn't have the money for a ticket. And it would be more fun with a friend. If he'd ever have one of those again.

ALONE TOGETHER

Travis continued on. The streets were busy with commuters. He heard horns and loud motors. He walked across an alleyway and a little dog started barking at him.

"Yeah, yeah, you don't want me around, either," he told the dog. The little dog just growled at him in response.

Travis finally grew tired. He settled at the local baseball park, where there was a field and a small playground. Recreational T-ball and Little League teams often practiced there. The park was where Travis would go with his dad to play Little League. Since it was during the school day, no teams were playing. However, there were some little kids playing on the playground equipment with their guardians watching nearby.

Travis sat under a tree and watched the little kids play on the structure. He remembered when he was that little, when his life had seemed so simple. He'd lived with both his parents together and he had a couple of friends. And all he thought about was playing outside, eating his favorite foods, and watching some cartoons. It was hard to imagine being that happy again as if it had all happened to another kid.

He watched a little boy run on the sidewalk toward his dad and fall down hard. He started to cry from scraping his knee. The father came to him and picked him up and gave him a hug. He watched the father talk to the boy as he wiped his tears. The father tried to make it all better.

Travis wished he could talk to his father about his problems, that his dad would help him make everything better again.

He wished he could tell him about the ghost.

Then they could discover the mystery together.

Travis blinked. Why couldn't he do that? Sure, his

dad might not believe him, but maybe it was time to have a real heart-to-heart with his dad. Travis was pretty exhausted dealing with everything on his own.

Maybe it was time to tell him about the ghost that was haunting him and how he was trying to discover his body to help him move on. And if that went well, he could be truthful to him about feeling so lonely. How everything had changed when Mom left. How sad he'd become and that he wished they'd spend more time together again.

Travis stood up and hurriedly walked home to talk to his dad.

Travis had stayed at the park longer than he thought. His dad might be really worried about him. What if the school had called about him missing the entire day?

Jeez, he didn't want his dad to be mad at him.

Travis spotted his dad's truck in the driveway and he knew he was likely in the backyard, working on the woodshop project. He had to tell him why he had been so distracted and hadn't been helping him with it. Instead of going through the house, he detoured through the backyard gate.

He rushed into the yard and stopped dead in his tracks.

He dropped his backpack from his hand and his mouth opened, but nothing came out.

The Mechanical Sunman was no longer nearly finished.

It was completely destroyed.

The cabinet was smashed into splintered pieces. The clump of wood that was for the automaton seemed to have been axed in half. Sawdust and small pieces of wood were scattered on the dry grass.

ALONE TOGETHER

The project that they had begun together was nothing but broken scraps.

But why?

His dad must have been angrier with Travis than he thought.

Travis had really let him down.

His hands began to shake and his bottom lip quivered. He wanted to cry. To yell. He wanted to pick up all the scraps of wood and throw them all over the yard. Everything seemed to be crashing down around him, and he felt like he didn't have control over anything. He didn't know what was going on at school or at home. He felt like everything was slipping out of his grasp as if he was trying to catch water.

The only tangible thing that had any real meaning was to find the ghost's body inside the cabinet. Maybe if he just found the body, everything would change and go back to being normal. As if finding the cabinet was the magical key to solving all his problems. He scanned his dad's worktable and spotted a small flashlight. He stuck it in his back pocket, and he spun around and just took off. He ran out of the yard. Ran as fast as he could. Tears burned his eyes and a lump formed in his throat.

He had to find the ghost's body.

Then his dad would have to understand why he hadn't been helping with the project. Why he'd been missing school. Why he wasn't acting like his usual self.

Once he found the ghost's body, his dad would have to understand. Then everything would be okay and he would love him again.

TALES FROM THE PIZZAPLEX

★ ★ ★

When Travis arrived to school, everyone was gone for the evening. He rattled the doors and found them locked up tight. He still hadn't checked the school attic or the storage sheds on the track field. He fell down on the ground, breathing heavily. He hadn't run that long and fast in a long time.

When he caught his breath, he knew the two sheds on the field were the only options at the moment. He shoved himself to his feet and headed for the field. He found the first shed easily enough. It was set to the right of the field and painted a bright red. He pulled the small flashlight from his pocket and flicked it on the shed's door. But when he went to open it, there was a large lock hanging from a chain on the door.

No.

Disappointed, Travis yanked at the chain, trying to see if he could loosen it, but the lock was too sturdy. He wasn't getting into this shed without a key. Maybe he could get in when they opened it for a PE class the next school day. But tomorrow seemed too late. There was an urgency drumming inside him.

He recalled the school map in his mind and scanned around for the other shed on the field. But he couldn't find it.

"That's weird," he murmured. He looked across the field to where the other shed should have been, but instead only spotted the old bleachers. "So where's the other shed?"

Travis started toward the bleachers. The school had upgraded to new seating, but instead of hauling out the the run-down benches, they moved them to the back of the field.

When Travis made his way over to the wood structure, he noticed some of the seats were broken and paint was chipping off the wood. Grass and weeds had overgrown underneath. There was some trash of used wrappers and soda cans stuck in the weeds.

Could the shed be hidden behind these bleachers? he wondered.

With the flashlight on, Travis squeezed underneath the back of the stacked benches and pushed aside the tall weeds.

Buried way in the very back was the other storage shed!

This one had faded red paint, with a rusted chain hanging from the door.

As Travis pushed through the weeds, he hoped he could at least get inside this shed. He rattled the rusted chain, and as if by some kind of miracle, the chain just fell off the door to the ground.

Yes! The door was blocked by thick weeds and it took a lot of shoving to wedge the door open enough to squeeze through.

It was pitch-dark inside and Travis walked into a spiderweb. He slapped it away and dropped the flashlight.

He felt a chill run across his body. Was the ghost around?

Travis leaped as he felt a spider skitter across his arm, He slapped at his skin and then he shoved himself against the back of the shed, breathing hard.

Sheesh! "Get it together, Travis," he whispered to himself. "Come on, you can't be scared now."

He couldn't let some creepy spiderwebs and insects scare him off. He had to get in there and search for the Mechanical Sunman.

He had this gut feeling that he was finally in the right place. That if there really was a body to be found, it would be here in this forgotten storage shed.

He took a breath and picked up the flashlight from the floor. He waited for his eyes to adjust to the darkness as he flashed the small beam of light across the shed. The storage area was nearly packed to the roof with junk.

"Jeez, that's a lot of stuff."

There were old nets filled with football jerseys and flags for flag football. There were rubber cones and footballs, soccer balls and Frisbees. Track hurdles and plastic mats. Hockey sticks and running batons. A couple of boxes piled with old wolf mascot costumes. There was a rusted push mower crammed in with other lawn stuff. It smelled of mildew and something rotten, like there may be some dead rodents in the shed.

Travis hesitated. *Or something else?*

The hairs on the back of his neck raised, and a burst of adrenaline flashed through him. He had to find out if the body was really there. If the ghost really died inside the cabinet.

He started grabbing at boxes and nets full of equipment in front of him and shoved them behind him. He threw the hockey sticks out of the way and pushed aside the hurdles. He was going to have to dig himself back out of the stuff but he didn't care. He needed to finish this. To find the truth. The ghost deserved to be found.

He threw stuff around and shoved through more. It started to become hard to breathe. Dust was flying everywhere and cobwebs stuck to his body.

He could do this.

ALONE TOGETHER

It felt like forever until he reached the back of the storage shed. His foot kicked something hard and Travis froze.

He reached out with his hand and he felt a large, wood box in front of him. His fingers actually tingled.

This had to be it!

He pulled off another cardboard box from atop the wood surface and scanned the flashlight onto the box.

And there it was, the unfinished Mechanical Sunman sitting on the cabinet!

He'd finally found it.

"You're here." He was starting to think he might never find it. "I feel like I've been looking for you forever." He touched the rough dents in the wood of the automaton's face. Travis could feel where the nose and the eyes were supposed to be.

It felt so surreal, as if he found a long-lost treasure.

"I found your Mechanical Sunman," he said aloud to the ghost. "Does that mean I really found you, too?"

His mouth went dry and he started to shiver. He brushed a hand across the surface. He felt a layer of dust brush off with his hand.

He crouched down in front of the cabinet. He grabbed the handles and tried to open the doors.

The doors were stuck.

Gritting his teeth, Travis yanked really hard but the cabinet wouldn't open. He then gripped the left handle with both hands.

The door jerked open and Travis fell backward.

He jerked upright.

There was no body.

He picked up the small flashlight he dropped and searched inside the space.

Aha! He found the missing library book he'd been looking for. The librarian must have been looking for this for a while. He pulled out the book and set it on top of the cabinet. It was dark inside and a putrid smell had him scrunching his nose. He admired the carpentry work. The wood was strong and sturdy. The cabinet space was a good size for a body to sit in. Curious, he crawled into the left side of the compartment and pulled his legs up to try to understand what could have happened to the ghost.

The cabinet door suddenly slammed shut!

Oh no, no, no!

Travis's eyes widened in shock. His lungs constricted in his chest.

The walls suddenly felt like they were closing in on him.

"No, please! Don't lock me in! I've been trying to help you! I've done everything to find the Mechanical Sunman for you!"

Sweat broke across his forehead. He hit the cabinet door and the wall beside him—hard—with his open palms in a panic, and then the wall beside him clicked and shifted down.

And there sitting next to him was the ghost's dead body!

Travis gasped and speared the light across the carcass. The boy's eyes were sunken into his skull. His skin was paper thin and glued to his bones. The muscles seemed to have shrunken away from the body. The mouth was gaping open, showing his teeth.

Travis screamed.

ALONE TOGETHER

★ ★ ★

Travis's heart pounded in his chest as his scream died off.

He tried to calm down. He needed to conserve his air and his energy. He shut his eyes for a moment and breathed slowly in and out through his nose.

"It's okay. I knew I would eventually find you. I mean, I was hoping. It's just not easy seeing a dead body for the first time."

He scanned the flashlight over the body. He was a typical kid who wore faded jeans and a T-shirt and old tennis shoes. He looked kind of small in the scrunched space, but it could be because the boy was slowly shrinking away.

Something strange caught Travis's eye. Something that had him frowning.

The boy wore a faded and frayed hat.

A weird feeling overcame him.

Unease. Uncertainty.

Something didn't feel right.

Travis reached out slowly, his fingers trembling.

He pulled the hat down on the boy's head so Travis could read the logo.

Fairhaven Park Little League.

Travis jerked his hand back, stunned. He dropped the flashlight.

That was Travis's hat. With exactly the same frayed edges and the hole in the bill.

"N-no. No, no, no."

This couldn't be right.

Travis shook his head and scooted against the back of the cabinet as if he could somehow get farther away from the truth. He pulled his legs against his chest, wrapped his arms around his knees, and stared at the body.

He studied the familiar jeans with the patch on the knee that his mother had mended for him, and he looked at the exact same jeans he was wearing. He scanned the plain white tee on the boy, and he realized their tees and tennis shoes matched, too.

Everything was exactly the same. Down to their discolored shoelaces.

The dead body . . .

. . . is my body.

The dead boy is . . . me!

As soon as his mind wrapped around the realization, something clicked.

It was as if a key finally fit perfectly into a lock and the gears shifted, opening up all his blocked memories.

Revealing the truth he hadn't been able to face until now.

He was the dead boy from inside the cabinet box.

He was the ghost that haunted Brighton Middle School.

The memories of Travis's life before he passed away flooded over him, and it was as if he was seeing his time as a ghost with a higher perspective. He'd been a shy seventh grader who liked to build things with his hands. He'd chosen to build the Mechanical Turk with the automaton as a Mechanical Sunman for woodshop class. His mom and dad were happily together at home, and Travis was eager to build this unique project all by himself. He'd told his parents that he was working on a special woodshop project at school, but he wanted to surprise them so he wasn't going to share any details until it was finished.

Travis was so excited. He wanted to show his dad how hard he worked on something all by himself. Travis wanted to make his dad proud of him.

He did the research, checked out the only book on the topic in the school library, hand drew all the sketches, and wrote down the notes in his woodshop notebook. He spent weeks building the intricate cabinet box with the hidden compartments. One day, when the Mechanical Sunman device was nearly finished, he figured he'd try it out. He still hadn't finished carving out the Sunman or making the mechanical instruments and gears to move the arms, but he was eager to see if he could fit comfortably inside the hidden compartments. He slipped into one side of the compartments in the cabinet right after school when Mr. Middlefield had left for the evening.

Travis closed the door, sealing himself inside.

He was pretty pleased with his results.

And then when he was ready to get out, the cabinet door wouldn't open.

Travis had cut the wood too precisely, and the door had become stuck.

He'd hit, he'd slapped, he'd kicked, he'd clawed at the wood. He'd called out for hours, but he'd made the cabinet too snug. Too airtight. Travis began to sweat and to lose air. As he tried to break into the next cabinet, he'd exhausted himself, and ultimately fell asleep to never wake up again.

Suddenly, he was just back at school. Completely forgetting that he'd died and going on with his life as if he was still alive, attending Brighton Middle School and continuing his seventh grade class schedule day after day.

That was why his lunch tab had stopped getting paid. Why there were no more rides in the Nova with his dad. No more having conversations at dinner. He'd noticed his mom and dad fighting, and he hadn't understood any of it.

He'd been so upset with their arguing that he'd slam the door closed to his room; they would hear it but were unable to see him or know that he was there with them in spirit.

Marissa was one of the rare gifted ones who could really see Travis. That was why she was so freaked out when he talked to her. Who wouldn't get freaked out by a talking ghost? Who wouldn't want to ignore one when you were trying to be normal? Travis didn't begrudge her one bit for not wanting to be friends with a dead kid who hadn't known he was actually dead.

Grandma had been home to finally speak with Travis because she had passed away peacefully in her sleep after Travis went missing. She met with Travis because he kept thinking of her, but in her heart, she knew he needed to find his own answers like she had.

His dad had built the mechanical automaton device in the backyard, without Travis. The notebook his dad had read from was Travis's old notebook.

The conversation his dad had on the phone with Travis's mom came clearly to him now.

". . . sometimes it feels like Travis is here with me . . . talking to me, telling me about his day. I know he could be out there somewhere, but in my heart, I believe he's gone.

"I even fix him dinner out of habit, so we can sit together . . . I know, I know, it's been two years, but I looked in his notes in his notebook. I started to build that woodshop project he last worked on before he disappeared. I thought it would make me feel better but it just brings back so much pain . . . I need to get rid of it."

So his dad had decided to break it all down.

"I'm actually gone," Travis spoke out loud.

Sad, Travis looked at his dead body before him, readjusting his Little League hat back up so he could see his sunken eyes a little bit better in the darkness. The body wasn't very scary after all, he decided. Travis had built the box airtight. No insects could penetrate the box, preserving Travis's body like a mummy.

It was just himself, a little shriveled up, but that was okay.

"I can't believe I didn't realize it for so long," he started to talk with himself. "It was like a part of me was missing, and it was you . . . or it was me." He shook his head, confused. "It doesn't matter now, because, you know, now we can be together. You won't be alone anymore and neither will I. We'll have each other always. Pretty cool, huh?"

Relieved, Travis settled in next to his corpse, and for the first time in a while, he didn't feel so alone anymore.

In fact, he would never feel alone again.

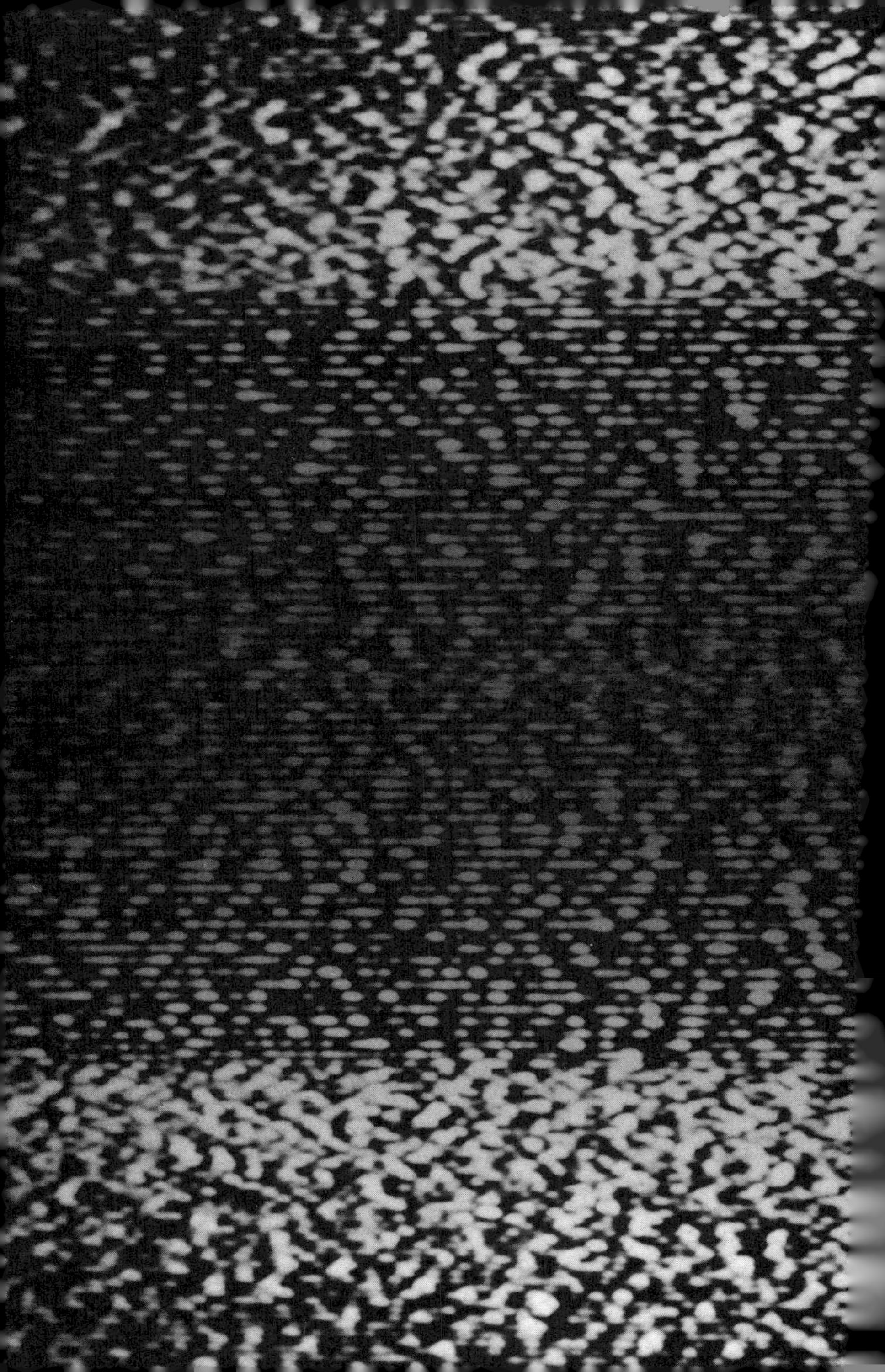

DITTOPHOBIA

RORY'S EYES SHOT OPEN. HIS BODY RIGID, HE STARED INTO THE MURKY GRAYNESS THAT PRESSED IN AROUND HIM. HE HELD HIS BREATH SO HE WOULDN'T MAKE A SOUND.

Rory's head and shoulders were propped on two puffy pillows that at the moment gave him no comfort at all. The room, though dim, was light enough that Rory could take in the closet door opposite the foot of his bed and his bedroom's two doorways, which faced each other from the left and the right of his bed. The pillows blocked his peripheral vision, so he couldn't see the small blue-gray nightstand that held his little red alarm clock with the two bells that looked like ears on top of the clock's face. Even so, Rory intuitively knew that it was just after midnight. He knew this because every night at about this time, the same thing happened: some small, unidentifiable noise—maybe a scrape or maybe a tap—woke him from a deep sleep. The noise woke him and then . . .

A flash of curved metal appeared in the gap between the white folding doors that enclosed Rory's closet. Rory sucked in a sharp breath. The whoosh of it was amplified in the stillness of the darkened room.

Oh no, Rory thought. *They know I'm awake.* He squeezed his eyes shut.

Rory had turned seven just a few months ago, although his memory of his small party—just him, his parents, and his friend, Wade, with the balloons and the big chocolate birthday cake he'd thought had too much icing—was so vague that it seemed like it had happened years ago instead of just weeks. However, as young as Rory was, he was old enough to know that closing his eyes wasn't a good defense against the creatures that were after him. Closed eyes weren't a force field. And they wouldn't make him invisible.

If Rory wanted to survive the night, he had to know what was coming. *Open your eyes!* he shouted at himself in his head.

He opened his eyes.

All the creatures appeared at once.

Once they came into view, the creatures moved slowly. That didn't make them any less scary. Rory kn from experience that the creatures' pace wouldn't make it easier for him to get away. He was never able to avoid them, no matter how slow they were.

Rory clutched his blankets and scooted up into a sitting position so that he could be poised to flee. But he didn't. Instead, he did what he always did when the monsters appeared. He froze and stared at them while his heart thumped faster and faster in his chest and cold sweat beaded on his forehead.

Rory didn't want to freeze. He wanted to spring from his bed and run, but for some reason he couldn't. All he could ever do when he first saw the creatures was watch them. Something about them held him suspended, like he was caught in a web.

From out of the closet, the piercingly sharp point of a pirate's hook scythed through the air as the rotting ruin of a fox-shaped creature with multiple rows of jagged teeth crept out into the room. The fox's eyes shone stark white in the surrounding darkness. Those eyes were focused directly on Rory.

Rory trembled. He tried—and failed—to keep himself from whimpering.

Two more pairs of eyes appeared, one set each in the open gaps of the doors to the left and the right of the bed. Two more creatures were preparing to slink toward Rory's bed.

Both doors opened wider. The creatures began to enter the room.

The creature on the right was a decayed version of a yellow chick, its body so riddled with holes that only the barest hints of a metal skeleton held it together. Like the fox, it had a massive mouth full of spiky teeth. Its lower jaw was so separated from its upper one that Rory could see the blue-gray pattern of his room's wallpaper through the space. Clutched in the chick's massive hand with long, razor-like nails was a bright pink cupcake with glowing white eyes and a smaller separated jaw full of serrated teeth. The cupcake, riding in the chick's big hand, was what entered the room first, slipping through the gloomy gap in the doorway that led to the right hallway outside Rory's room. The fact that the cupcake was a cupcake and had a smaller mouth made it no less terrifying. When the cupcake opened and closed its jaw, it made a snapping sound that raised goose bumps on Rory's skin.

The creature coming from the left was similar to the other two in its decomposing awfulness and its pointy teeth and nails. The nails were the first thing Rory could see as the creature slowly slipped its hand past the edge of the door and stepped into the room. This creature was a monstrous distortion of a purple-blue bunny, complete with long, mottled bunny ears that rose above its oversize open-mouthed face. The fact that this monster was bunny-like made it the worst of the three for Rory because he loved bunnies. This monster showed him that even the best of things could be contorted and wrecked, twisted into something ugly and gross.

The creatures made a clacking and burring sound when they walked, but they moved smoothly, almost like they were floating. They weren't floating, though. When the creatures were in motion, Rory's room shook. The walls rattled, and Rory's bed vibrated. Or maybe his bed felt like it was vibrating because he was quivering.

Although most of Rory was stone-still, his teeth were chattering.

As the creatures approached the bed, the *puff-puff-puff* of heavy breathing filled the room. The panting inhales and exhales, however, weren't coming from the creatures. Rory was the one making all that racket. The creatures, except for their clunking steps, made very little sound. Their movement created the faintest of chinks and whirs and the occasional creak, and somehow the fact that they didn't barrel at Rory with loud roars or bellows made them all that more horrid. The near silence of their advance gave Rory too much time to imagine what they would do to him when they reached him.

And they'd reached him.

Rory felt his mattress shift. His gaze whipped to the left. The monster bunny was pressed against the foot of the bed. The bunny was leaning forward. He was reaching for Rory.

Finally, Rory could move. It felt like he'd been released from a tractor beam.

Rory launched himself out of the bed, on the right, squinting toward the advancing chick. He was pretty sure he could scamper past it and . . .

A mutilated brown bear with even larger teeth than those of the other creatures shot up from beneath Rory's bed and blocked his escape. The bear wore a black top hat and a black bow tie. Neither gentlemanly accessory made the bear any less gruesome. With a raspy rumble, the bear's mouth hinged wider and wider. It leaned toward Rory.

Cold metal clamped around Rory's wrist. Hot pain pierced his skin. Rory screamed.

DITTOPHOBIA

★ ★ ★

Rory sat up. His chest heaving, he gripped the edge of the quilt that lay atop his tangled sheets and blankets. Sweat trickled down his neck. His cotton pajamas clung to his skin. Rory's heartbeat sounded like a full drum set pounding out an impossibly fast riff that filled the room.

His eyes wide, Rory jerked his head left and right. The creatures were gone.

So was the night.

Through the shades covering the window high up above the head of Rory's bed, bright sunlight streamed into the room. Morning was here. The nightmare was over.

Even if Rory had looked up toward the window, he knew he wouldn't see the sun. The window was well above any height he could reach, and it was covered with a shade that let in light but hid any potential view that might be seen by a very tall person. Rory never understood why his room's window was so close to the ceiling, but he'd gotten used to it.

Rory leaned forward and scanned the space around him. In the warm yellow light, the bedroom looked cheerful and friendly. But Rory was still tense. He studied his surroundings carefully.

Nothing looked out of place. His blue-gray furniture—a tall chest of drawers, which held a purple three-bladed fan and the lava lamp his uncle had given him, and a shorter dresser that held a yellow porcelain lamp with a gray-striped shade—was placed where it always was. Both pieces of furniture sat against Rory's lavender-gray and white wallpapered walls. The wallpaper in Rory's room covered only the top two-thirds or so of the walls; below the wallpaper, there was something called a chair rail. (Rory's mom was an interior decorator, and she made sure he knew what things in houses were called.) A chair rail was molding on the wall that divided the upper wallpaper from a different kind of wallpaper—in Rory's room, it was gray and blue striped—that covered the wall between the chair rail and the floor. Whenever Rory walked past the molding, it was about the level of his chest. Rory was four and a half feet tall, so he knew that meant the molding was about three and a half feet off the floor.

The tall chest sat against the wall opposite Rory's bed; it was next to the double-doored closet. The dresser was on the right wall, next to the doorway that led out to the hallway that went past his parents' room before reaching the living room. The white six-paneled door was closed. So was the matching door on the other side of the room. That door led to another hall, which also went to the living room. Rory's bathroom and two other rooms opened off that left-side hall.

Staring at his folding closet door, Rory noticed it was closed, too. He always made sure it was closed before he went to bed. The door was louvered (according to his mom). Rory wished it wasn't. The open slats of the louvers made the closet far too exposed to suit Rory. He knew what lived in that closet, and he wished he had solid doors he could keep closed. And locked.

But would a solid, locked door help? The two hallway doors were solid, and Rory always made sure they were closed and locked. Even so, the creatures always got the doors open. Every single night.

He shook himself. He blew out air.

"They're just nightmares," he told himself. His voice sounded unnaturally loud in the room.

DITTOPHOBIA

Rory's voice seemed loud, he thought, because it was the only sound in the room. His bedroom was otherwise silent. No, not quite silent. A barely there hissing sound came from vents in the ceiling above Rory's bed. He glanced up at them. The rectangular grate-covered vents looked as they always did. His mom thought ceiling vents were ugly, but the vents didn't bother Rory. He'd never seen anything bad come through the vents. The hissing sound was very soft, like a steady whisper. Rory thought the sound was soothing.

Rory threw back his quilt, looked down at the purple-gray carpet that covered his bedroom floor, and tentatively hung his legs over the side of the bed. Feeling prickles at the bottom of his feet, Rory quickly dropped to his knees on the floor and looked under the bed. Nothing was there.

Rory pushed himself up and stood. He looked around again.

Even though he'd probably get in trouble for it, he'd left a few toys scattered around the floor of his room. A blue telephone with large googly eyes and red wheels sat contentedly next to a green plastic fish near the chest of drawers. A few feet from the rolling phone, a purple robot was hanging out in front of the dresser. Between the telephone and the robot, a rabbit stood up straight a few feet from the closet doors.

The sight of the rabbit made Rory uneasy. He whipped his head away from it and sat down on the edge of his bed. He clenched the white fabric of his quilt and looked at the hand-sewn triangles that were patchworked together with the white material. The triangles had many patterns—some looked like circles and some were leaf or flower shaped; all the patterns shared the same colors of blue, beige, and yellow. Rory's grandma and some of her friends had made the quilt for him. His mom said the quilt didn't match the colors in his room, but he didn't care. He liked it.

Glancing at the rabbit again, Rory called out, "Mom!"

When his mom didn't answer, he tried, "Dad!"

His dad didn't respond, either.

His parents were probably getting ready for work and didn't hear him. Rory shrugged. He should stop being a weirdo and get ready for school.

Standing, Rory shuffled, barefooted, to the door on the left side of the room. He hesitated only a second before gripping the door's brass knob, opening the door, and stepping out into the hallway.

Rory looked left and right along the length of the wood-floored hall. Like his room, the hall had the chair rail thing and two different wallpapers. The paper above the rail was kind of burgundy-orange with a fancy diamond-shaped pattern. The paper below was a dark grayish-brown with splotches of lighter gray in sort of treeish shapes. Rory didn't like either of the wallpapers, but he figured they probably looked better than he thought they did. His mom was an expert at decorating houses; she must have known what looked good and what didn't.

Nothing was in the hall other than a small hall table with one drawer. A lamp similar to the one in Rory's room, this one in the color of a pale pumpkin, sat on the table.

Rory crossed the hall and went into the bathroom. The wood floor felt cool and hard under his bare feet.

DITTOPHOBIA

Somehow the bathroom had escaped his mom's love of wallpaper. It was painted light blue, and its tiled floor was dark blue and white striped. The big bathtub with feet like a creature's claws (Rory didn't like the claws) was white, and so was the sink and toilet.

Rory used the toilet and then stood in front of the sink to wash his hands and brush his teeth. After he did these things that he was supposed to do every morning, he lifted his face and looked straight ahead so he could check his hair in the mirror.

He didn't much care about his hair, or the rest of what he looked like, but Rory's mom did. She was always telling him to comb his hair.

Rory looked around the sink for his comb but couldn't find it. He did his best to smooth his short hair with his fingers but it didn't want to lay down. The dark-blondish waves (his mom said his hair looked like a hay field on a rainy day), stuck out from his head in multiple directions. His hair stood out even farther than his big ears, which poked out from the sides of his narrow head. (Wade once suggested that Rory file the tops of his ears into peaks so he could be an elf. Rory thought that was really stupid.)

Giving up on trying to get his hair under control, Rory bent over and sloshed water on his face. Straightening again, he used a blue towel to wipe the water off the mass of freckles that covered his wide cheekbones and slightly pointy nose. Rory noticed the skin around the freckles was paler than usual. He also saw that the skin under his eyes was darker than the rest of his face. The whites around his greenish-brown eyes were streaked with spider-webby red lines. He tried to smile to reassure himself that he didn't look as bad as he thought he did, but baring all the small, white teeth in his wide mouth made his head and face look like a crazy jack-o'-lantern. He closed his mouth and left the bathroom.

Returning to his bedroom, Rory shed his pajamas and put on jeans and a green T-shirt. Both the jeans and the T-shirt were baggy.

Rory wasn't a big kid; he was smaller than most of the boys in his class. His mom, however, kept expecting him to start "a growing spurt," so she bought him clothes that were too large. Rory hoped his mom was right. Rory's dad loved football, and Rory wanted to get big so he could play. Rory could remember tossing a football back and forth with his dad, but the memory was hazy. They hadn't done it in a long time.

He stuffed his feet into socks and pulled on a pair of navy blue sneakers. Rory left his room again, this time through the door on the right.

The hallway to the right of Rory's room was the same as the one on the left. His parents' room, a bathroom, and one other room opened off this hall. All three rooms' doors were closed.

Rory tried calling out to his parents again. "Mom! Dad!"

Once more, he got no answer.

Rory walked down the hall. Because his sneakers had rubber bottoms, Rory's footfalls on the wood floor weren't loud. His footsteps were a quiet shuffle tap. He could easily hear the other sounds in the house. He paused outside the bathroom door. Through the door, he could hear the sound of a running shower. "Mom!" he yelled out.

She didn't respond.

DITTOPHOBIA

Keeping his eyes closed so he wouldn't see anything he wasn't supposed to, Rory gripped the doorknob. He figured if he opened the door and yelled again, his mom would hear him.

He took a deep breath. Expecting to inhale the scent of soap or shampoo coming from the bathroom, Rory was surprised when he smelled something sharper—something like medicine. He shrugged and shouted for his parents one more time. He still got no response.

"Whatever," he mumbled.

His dad must have already gone to work. He went to work early a lot.

His mom was probably thinking hard about some decorating project while she showered, and that was why she didn't hear him. She was always thinking about her work. Even when Rory talked to her, he could tell she was thinking about her work. As he talked, her gaze would drift off to the side, and he could tell that she wasn't interested in what he was saying. He guessed that was normal, though. Mostly, he talked about his friend, Wade, and their clubhouse. That was probably boring to his mom.

With his dad gone and his mom lost in thought in the shower, Rory was on his own. Well, what was new about that?

Rory went down the hall and stepped into what his mom called their great room. This part of the house was open concept. That meant that the living room and dining room were one big space. Off to the side of those areas, a big island with wood stools divided the large space from a kitchen filled with shiny appliances and white cabinets.

Passing a long, rectangular, dark-colored wood dining table with six dark-blue plush chairs, Rory went around the island and walked to the end of the kitchen. That's where the fridge was. He was hungry, and his mom hadn't yet set anything out on the island for breakfast.

When it came to what he liked to eat, Rory was—in his mom's opinion—a strange kid. Rory guessed she was right. All the kids in Rory's class loved sweet things. They were always talking about how much they liked candy and ice cream, and he knew they ate sugary cereals or waffles or donuts for breakfast. Rory didn't like sweet stuff. For breakfast, he liked having fruit and bagels with cream cheese.

Rory reached for the sleek vertical silver handle on the stainless-steel fridge. He knew he'd have to wipe his finger smudges from the handle after he got his food. His mom was obsessed about smudges on her appliances.

Opening the fridge, Rory wrinkled his nose. The inside of the fridge smelled stale, like the bread had gone bad. Or was it the cream cheese? Rory grabbed a bagel from a bag on the lower shelf and opened the cheese drawer to get out a carton of spreadable cream cheese. He frowned. They didn't have any cream cheese.

Rory shrugged. He'd have to remind his mom to buy some cream cheese.

Opening the lower produce drawer, Rory grabbed a pear. The pear was browner than it should have been and maybe a little softer than what was best for a pear, but Rory figured it would be all right, too.

Closing the fridge door, Rory cradled the bagel and the pear, and he used the back of his free hand to wipe a smudge off the fridge door handle. Then he carried everything to the island.

Grabbing a paper towel off the roll by the big white sink, Rory returned to the island and spread out the paper towel on the island's gray granite counter. His mom always nagged him about using plates, but he didn't like to mess with dishes. The only thing he ever washed was the small glass he used for water when he got thirsty during the day. He always rinsed that glass and kept it by the sink.

Climbing up onto one of the stools, Rory set his bagel and pear on the paper towel. He lifted the bagel and smelled it. It might have been a little old, but it looked okay. He took a hesitant bite of the bagel. He quirked his lips as he chewed. The bagel was dry, but it wasn't terrible.

Rory reached for the pear and bit into it. It, too, wasn't at its best, but it was okay.

As he ate, Rory listened for his mom. She had to be out of the shower by now, didn't she?

Apparently not. Rory could still hear the shushing-crackle of the shower's running water.

Rory finished his breakfast and cleaned up after himself, making sure he left no crumbs on the counter. His mom was as obsessive about crumbs as she was about smudges on stainless steel.

As he put his trash in the bin under the kitchen sink, Rory suddenly realized he was going to be late for school if he didn't get moving.

Hurrying out of the kitchen, Rory spotted his red backpack next to the end of the blue-and-white-checked sofa in the living room part of the great room. Good thing he'd left his backpack there so he didn't have to take the time to go back to his room.

Rory picked it up and slipped it over his shoulders. He hurried across the living room's wood floor toward the—

He stopped.

Where was the front door?

Turning in a full circle, Rory frowned as he tried to find the door that would lead out of the house. For some reason, he couldn't remember where it was supposed to be.

The living room, like most of the rest of the house, had two different wallpapers separated by another chair rail. The paper in here had vertical stripes of bright blue and white above the rail; these colors matched the sofa and the rectangular rug under the oval coffee table in front of the sofa. Below the rail, wider vertical stripes of beige and cream colors matched his dad's recliner and a TV cabinet. A couple paintings and two groupings of family photos hung on the blue-and-white part of the walls. The rest of the walls were bare, but for a couple of windows covered with cloth shades. The shades were thin enough that daylight shone through them, but they were thick enough to make it impossible to see through to the outside.

He didn't care about seeing through the windows, though. He wanted a door, not a window.

Rory walked around the entire living room and dining room area. As he did, his brain started getting a little mushy. With every step he took, he felt a little drowsier. By the time he had gone around the room twice, he felt like he was in a fog.

Why couldn't he find his way out of his house?

And where was his mom?

Rory adjusted his backpack on his shoulders. He headed back down the hall toward his parents' bedroom.

When he reached the other room off the hall leading to his parents' room, Rory tried its door. Just as he couldn't remember where the door was in the great room, he couldn't remember what was in this room, either. He wasn't going to find out now, though. The handle jiggled but the door wouldn't open. It was locked.

Rory walked on and paused in front of his parents' door. From there, he could still hear the shower in the bathroom. Maybe his dad hadn't left for work, though. Perhaps his dad had slept in or something.

"Dad?" Rory called out. "Are you in there?"

When his dad didn't answer him, Rory put his ear to the door. The painted wood felt smooth and cool against his ear.

Rory's ear, however, didn't give him any information. He heard nothing.

Knowing he shouldn't just barge into his parents' room but wishing he could find his mom or dad, Rory gripped the door handle and tried to turn it. Like the one on the other room's door, the knob wiggled a little but the door wouldn't open.

Rory stepped a few feet forward and tried the bathroom door again. The door wouldn't give. Behind the door, the sound of the shower continued.

Rory looked down the hall. Was there a back door out of the house somewhere? He couldn't remember a back door off this hall, but then he couldn't remember his house not having a door at all, either.

He wandered down the hall. It ended just past the doorway to his bedroom, and there was a door there.

Rory tried to open it. Like the other doors he'd tried, this one remained closed. He tried a little harder to get this one open, but no matter how much he rattled the knob and shoved at the door's hard surface, it didn't give at all.

Rory shrugged. He didn't think this was a door that led outside anyway. It was probably the door to a closet. A closet wouldn't help him.

Rory turned around and headed back down the hall. Going into his bedroom through its right-side door, he looked around. His bed was still mussed, his pillows askew against the slatted wood headboard. His mom wouldn't like it if she saw that he hadn't made his bed.

Rory went to the head of his bed and pulled up the sheets and blankets. He smoothed them out, put the pillows in their right places at the head of the bed, and then pulled the quilt up to cover everything. Patting the quilt, he nodded.

"That's better," he said.

Once again, his words sounded unusually loud. And behind the boom of his voice, the steady hissing above his bed sounded like a subdued murmur, as if someone—maybe Rory's mom?—was saying "Shhh," letting him know everything was okay.

Rory smiled dreamily. "Everything's okay," he told himself. This time when he spoke, he made sure to keep his voice low.

Walking through his room, Rory exited it through the left-side door. Looking to his left in the hallway, he spotted another door at the end of it. Was that a back door that led outside?

DITTOPHOBIA

Rory took a couple steps to the door and tried to turn the knob. It was just like all the other knobs Rory had attempted to turn. It shifted just a tiny bit but wouldn't rotate to open the door.

He turned around and put his back to the locked door. He went back down the hall toward the great room.

Although the bathroom door was open as Rory had left it earlier, the other two doors along this hall were closed. They were also locked. He moved on past them, and then he was back in the great room again.

Rory stopped there near the dining room table. He shifted the weight of his backpack on his back.

He felt like he was missing something. He had to have been. He should have been able to pick up his backpack and leave the house to go to school. That should have been a simple thing. Shouldn't it?

Not sure what else to do, Rory walked through the house again.

And again.

Feeling disoriented and a little loopy, like he was just on the edge of falling asleep but not quite there yet, Rory paced through his house over and over. He was so caught up in his quest to find a door that he lost track of time. He couldn't tell if time was passing slowly or quickly, and he didn't care. He just wanted to find the door so he could go to school.

On a pass through the great room, Rory noticed that the room was darker than it had been the last time he'd walked through it. He glanced at the windows.

The shades over the windows weren't the nice bright yellow color they'd been when the sun had been out.

They were turning a dingy gray. Daylight was fading. In fact, it was nearly gone.

"Time for bed," Rory said to himself.

Good, he thought. He was so tired. He was more than ready to get under the covers and snuggle into his nice, warm bed.

Rory shrugged out of his backpack. He dropped it near the end of the blue-and-white-checked sofa, turned, and walked down the hall to the bathroom. He was tired, but he didn't want to go to bed without a shower.

Stripping out of his clothes in the bathroom, Rory curled his hand around the chrome knob that jutted from the white tile that surrounded the tub. For a second, he was afraid to turn the knob. Every knob he'd turned today had refused to budge.

His eyes heavy and his limbs getting even heavier, Rory sighed at his silliness. He turned the knob. The shower spray cascaded down into the tub. The rushing sound was reassuring.

The sound reminded him of his mom's shower. He couldn't remember if he'd heard the shower the last time that he'd gone down the right-side hall. He must not have. His mom must have left for work when Rory was in the left-side hall. She would have figured that he'd already gone to school, so she wouldn't have gone looking for him.

Rory took a quick shower. He brushed his teeth. Then he gathered his clothes and trotted into his room. Closing and locking the door behind him, Rory crossed his room and closed and locked the other door as well. Then he put on his favorite pjs—they were black-and-white zebra striped.

DITTOPHOBIA

By now, Rory's room was lit only by the weak glow of his nightstand lamp, a smaller version of the lamp on top of his dresser. The little lamp threw a faint circle of light out around his bed. Beyond that circle, the rest of the room was in shadows. All the shapes that squatted in those shadows suddenly looked dangerous and threatening.

Rory quickly went to his closet door. He tossed his clothes into a blue plastic laundry basket on the floor and then closed the door firmly. He scuttled to his bed, threw back the quilt and other covers, and dove under them. He pulled the covers up to his chin and looked around the room.

The lumpy shapes in the room made Rory nervous. But at least none of them moved. Yet.

Rory risked slipping an arm from beneath his covers to turn off his bedside lamp. He closed his eyes, letting the steady hiss from the vents lull him to sleep as the drowsiness he'd felt all day finally claimed him.

Rory's eyes shot open.

It was midnight again, he was sure. Or close enough.

A skirring sound came from the closet at the other end of the room. Rory lifted his head from the pillow very slowly. He raised his head only an inch, if that. He blinked several times, willing his eyes to adjust to the room's darkness. He had to see what the sound was.

The closet door was cracked open.

He'd closed it before he'd gone to bed. Hadn't he?

Rory watched the gap. He stared so hard, so unblinkingly, that his eyes started to sting. But he didn't blink. If he did, he might miss it if the door opened farther.

157

Don't blink.

Don't blink.

He blinked.

As he opened his eyes again, he caught the tip of the gleaming metal hook curling around the edge of the closet door. He heard a metallic rasp. The door creaked. A pair of glowing white eyes looked through the crack between the closet doors.

No.

Rory checked the doors that led out to the hallways that flanked his room. He'd closed them, too; he was positive about that.

They weren't closed now. Knifelike nails curled around the edges of the doors. One blazing white eye peered through each opening.

As Rory watched, trying to control the shudders that wanted to wrack his body, both doors opened even more. One eye in each doorway became two. Now four eyes stared at him from the open doors. No, six. Rory could see a smaller set of radiant white eyes lower down in the right-side gap. It was the murderous cupcake with the gaping mouth full of teeth.

Rory kept watching. What else could he do? He couldn't move, even though he wanted to run more than anything.

The closet door and the hall doors opened wider. The gigantic mouths full of sharklike teeth appeared. The tattered bodies wormed into view. Zombielike versions of a fox, a chick, and a bunny began to plod toward Rory's bed.

Run! Rory's mind screamed at him.

DITTOPHOBIA

Finally, Rory was able to get his body to work. He threw back his covers. He sprang from his bed.

Before Rory could take a step, however, another pair of gleaming eyes was suddenly right in front of him. Beneath the eyes, another cavern of a mouth full of pointy teeth opened. The teeth were inches from Rory's face.

Rory shrieked.

Rory opened his eyes and blinked at the sun's glaring rays. Wiping sweat from his forehead, he wrinkled his nose at the musky stench of his body. His skin felt wet and sticky. His pajamas were twisted around him, and they clung to him.

Lying still and scanning the room, Rory concentrated on breathing slowly and evenly. The sound of his quiet, controlled breathing relaxed the tightness in his muscles. He continued to focus on his inhales and exhales.

As he listened to himself breathe, Rory realized that the sound of his breathing was a gentle percussion beneath the steady whisper coming from above him. Rory looked up. Right. The vents. Their usual hiss comforted Rory.

The night was over. All was well.

Or was it?

Rory sat up. His hands balled into fists, he looked around the room.

Everything was as it should have been. Both his hall doors and his closet door were closed.

Rory swung his legs out of the bed. "Mom!" he called. "Dad!"

Rory's parents didn't respond. He shrugged and went to his closet.

At the double louvered doors, he paused. His nightmare was niggling at the edges of his consciousness. He was afraid to open the doors.

"There's nothing there," he told himself.

Rory's voice bounced off the room's walls and came back at him like a punch in the face. He shook his head and made himself open the closet doors.

Everything in the closet was what was supposed to be in the closet. There was nothing scary in sight.

Rory realized his shoulders were nearly up by his ears. He relaxed them. He looked down and discovered his hands were out in front of him, as if he was getting ready to ward off an attack. He dropped his hands.

Rory gathered his clothes, closed his closet, and left his room to go into the bathroom. He examined his pinched face in the mirror. Was he paler than he should have been?

Rory rolled his eyes. He was fine. Who cared what color his skin was?

Going back into his room, Rory made his bed. Then he left his room through the right-side door. He headed down the hall and called for his parents again. When they didn't answer, he concluded that his dad was at work and his mom was in the shower. He could hear the shower running through his parents' bathroom door.

"Same ol', same ol'," Rory said to himself, chuckling. His dad usually went to work early. His mom took very long showers.

It wasn't a problem. Rory was used to fending for himself.

Making his way down the hall, through the great room, and into the kitchen, Rory scrounged up some breakfast. He grabbed a bagel that seemed a little harder than it should have been and a peach that was a little softer than he wanted it to be.

When Rory finished his breakfast, he tried one last time to call out to his mom. "Mom! You out of the shower yet?"

She didn't answer him. Maybe she'd gotten out of the shower and left for work while he was eating. His mom often told him that when he was eating, he wouldn't notice an elephant if it sat down next to him.

Rory grinned at the idea of a visiting elephant as he pulled on his backpack and headed toward the—

Where was the front door?

Rory frowned and turned in a full circle. How could he have forgotten where the door was?

Rory rubbed his eyes. They felt dry and droopy.

Shaking off a sudden sense of sleepiness, Rory walked around the edges of the great room, trailing his hand along the chair rail as he went. He wasn't sure why he was doing that. It wasn't like the door was going to be invisible or something. But he kept slipping his hand along the chair rail, and when he finished going around the great room, he kept his hand on the chair rail as he went down the hall toward his parents' room. He wiggled the doorknob on every closed door he came to. None of the doors opened.

Rory tried calling out to his parents again, even though he knew that was pointless. They were at work. Or was his mom still in the shower? Rory could hear the shower running, so she must have been. Either that or she'd forgotten to turn off the shower. If she'd done that, she'd be annoyed when she got home and realized how much water she'd wasted.

By the time the light shining through the shades in the great room began to fade, Rory wasn't sure how many times he'd gone through the house. A dozen? More? The whole time he traipsed through the house, he had a powerful sense that something was getting past him. There was something he should have noticed. Something he should have done differently. But he didn't know what it was.

When the house began to fill with puddles of darkness, Rory got ready for bed. Making sure he closed his closet door and the doors to the hallways, he got into bed. By then, Rory was so tired that he could barely stay awake long enough to turn off his lamp. Once he switched it off, Rory pulled up the covers and closed his eyes. He was asleep immediately.

Rory's eyes shot open.

The creatures came at midnight. Like always. They somehow got the doors open. They skulked into the room. They closed in around Rory's bed. White eyes. Saw-toothed mouths. Decomposing bodies. *Clankety-clank.*

Rory tried to get away. That's when the fourth creature appeared. The bear with the top hat drew itself up to loom over Rory as if arising from a grave under Rory's bed. Mouth opening impossibly wide, the bear aimed its teeth at Rory's head.

Rory's cry jolted him awake.

As soon as his eyes opened, Rory was blinded by the sun. He didn't, however, close his eyes against it. He was grateful for the brightness. It was what made it possible for him to look around the room and assure himself that nothing was in his room besides what was supposed to be there. He was alone. He was safe.

Rory called for his mom and dad, but they didn't answer. Rory could hear the sound of a shower running, even over the hiss of air flowing from the vents above his bed. He figured his mom was in the shower. She showered a lot. His dad was probably at work. Rory was amazed at how much his dad worked. Didn't his dad ever get tired?

Rory wished he saw his dad more. And his mom, too. She worked almost as much as his dad. It seemed like Rory was alone a lot. That was okay, though. He was used to it.

Rory went into the bathroom and washed away the sweat from the previous night. He brushed his teeth and gave in to his hair's need to stick out around his head like he was a porcupine instead of a boy.

After he dressed, Rory went into the kitchen to get some breakfast. When Rory looked in the fridge, he discovered there weren't any bagels. Bagels were his favorite breakfast food. But wheat toast was okay. The wheat bread was in the fridge, and it looked a little moldy. Rory figured he could scrape off the mold, though. He also found an apple. The apple was a little shriveled; otherwise, it looked okay. Rory wished he had some peanut butter for his bread, but he couldn't find any. He ended up eating the bread plain. It was dry, but it tasted all right. So did the apple, although it wasn't as crisp as Rory wanted it to be.

As soon as he was done with breakfast, Rory knew he was going to be late for school if he didn't hurry. Rushing through the great room, he snatched up his backpack from the floor by the sofa. Slipping it onto his back, he started toward the—

Where was the front door?

Rory frowned and looked around. He saw the usual furniture and wallpaper and the windows with the shades that let in the light but didn't let Rory see outside. He didn't, however, see a door. Where'd the door go?

Feeling fuzzy like he'd stayed up too late, Rory began making his way through the house, looking for the door. A couple times, he called out to his mom in case she was still here. She never answered. She had to have gone to work, either while Rory had been in the bathroom or while he'd been concentrating on getting his breakfast. When Rory had been a little younger, his mom had taken him to school, but now he walked on his own. His mom was often so focused on her work that she left without remembering to say good-bye to him.

Rory made a circuit through the house. When he couldn't find the door, the only thing he could think to do was take another pass through the house. So, he started over and went down the hall toward his parents' room again.

Halfway down the hall, Rory stopped. He listened carefully.

Rory was familiar with the normal noises in his house. He was used to hearing a hiss from the vents and the hum of the refrigerator's motor. Because his mom took so many showers that were really long, he well knew the sound of continually running water, too.

Now, though, Rory could hear something else. It

surprised him. It was a noise he'd never heard before in his house.

The noise was a knocking sound, and it was coming from inside one of the walls. Which one? Rory couldn't tell.

The knocking sound wasn't a knocking like a person would do. There wasn't some little trapped fairy or something in the walls. (Although the idea of that made Rory smile.)

No. The knocking Rory heard was like the clunking sound an engine might make if it was having trouble running. It was like a heavy chugging sound wrapped in a sharp thunk. Rory was just starting to learn about cars, so he didn't know a lot about engines. From what little he knew, though, he thought what he was hearing sounded like an engine's pistons misfiring. The bangs in the wall sounded like an engine about to fail.

Rory walked along the hallway, his ear to the wall. He listened, and he thought about what he was hearing. He couldn't make sense of it. Why would there be an engine in the walls?

The sound stopped just as abruptly as it had started. When it stopped, though, everything stopped. Well, almost everything. The hissing stopped. The sound of the shower stopped. The only thing that continued was the refrigerator's hum. Other than that, the house went silent. The only other sound besides the refrigerator that Rory could hear was that of his own breathing and his own footsteps.

Rory stood still and listened. Nope. Nothing else.

"That's weird," Rory said.

He didn't care much about it, though. He was so tired. He could barely keep his eyes open.

The last time he'd been in the great room, the sun had no longer been shining through the shades anyway. It was time for bed.

Rory went into the bathroom and showered; then he went to his room, closed all his doors, and got into bed. He was asleep as soon as he turned out his light.

Rory's eyes shot open. He squinted into the sun's perky yellow rays. He watched little specks of dust dance in the stream of light that slanted down over his bed, and he stretched his arms above his head. He felt great.

Rory dropped his arms back to his sides and took in a big breath of air. He wiggled his legs and flexed his toes. He felt different from how he usually felt in the morning. Why?

The answer came quickly.

No nightmares. Rory hadn't dreamed at all. He'd slept peacefully through the night. The creatures hadn't come.

Rory frowned. No, it wasn't just that. It was something else, too.

Rory sat up and looked around his room. He gasped.

What had happened to his room?

Although the room Rory was in was still clearly his room, with its blue-gray furniture and lavender-gray and white wallpaper and white doors and purple-gray carpet and scattering of toys, it definitely wasn't his room as he remembered it. Something was wrong.

Yesterday, everything in Rory's room had been clean and nice. Today, everything was dirty—really dirty. And it wasn't nice. Not at all.

DITTOPHOBIA

The wallpaper, for one thing, was peeling off the walls. Wide strips of the wallpaper above the chair rail were drooping down over it. The strips were crusty, and the backside of them were yellow. The wallpaper below the chair rail was peeling off the wall, too. Some of it had fallen onto the carpet.

The carpet was in awful shape as well. It was filthy. A thick coating of dust looked like a layer of fuzz. The fuzz was disturbed by a jumble of footprints. Rory leaned forward and stared at the prints. They were big, even bigger than his large feet. Had the creatures left the prints?

Rory's gaze flitted to the closet door. He frowned. One of the closet doors was sagging off its hinges. The other one was bent. Both closet doors were covered with dust.

Rory looked left and right at the other two doors. They were dingy and dusty, too, but they were closed.

Realizing that he needed to pee, Rory had to set aside the mystery of what had happened to his room. He reached down to push his quilt back.

Rory's hands froze. He looked at the quilt. It was no longer white; it was so dirty it was almost brown. The material of the quilt was thin, too, and the triangular patches were coming apart from one another.

Well, Rory would worry about that later. He needed to get into the bathroom.

Rory swung his legs over the side of the bed. Once again, he froze.

Rory stared down at his bare legs. Where were his pajamas? And why were his legs so long? And furry? Where did the hair come from?

Panicked, Rory shouted, "Mom!"

The sound of Rory's voice nearly made him fall off the bed. *Mom* came out in a deep tone that sounded more like his dad's voice than his own. What had happened to Rory?

Rory's mom didn't answer, and Rory's need for the toilet was now more important than anything. Rory pushed off the bed and stood. He now towered over the bed. Rory's stomach flipped over as he ran toward the door to the hallway. His breathing came out in rapid bursts as he grabbed the doorknob. That's when he saw his hand. His hand was at least twice the size he remembered it being. The knob disappeared beneath his broad palm and his long fingers.

Big hand or not, though, Rory still needed to pee. He flung the door open and dashed across the hall to the bathroom. Even as he made a beeline for the toilet, he noticed that the chair rail was now below his waist level instead of near his chest.

Rory was practically hyperventilating by the time he flushed the toilet. He was almost afraid to turn toward the mirror, but he had to.

Rory stepped up to the sink and looked into the mirror. His mouth dropped open, and his eyes widened. The image in the mirror gaped back at him.

Both Rory and the guy in the mirror opened their mouths wider and screamed, "Mom!"

Neither Rory nor the guy in the mirror received a reply. So, they kept staring at each other.

Was the guy in the mirror as in awe of Rory as Rory was of the guy in the mirror?

Rory leaned forward. So did the guy in the mirror.

DITTOPHOBIA

The last time Rory remembered looking in the mirror—wasn't that just yesterday?—he'd looked into the brownish-green eyes of a skinny boy. The boy Rory remembered had a narrow face with freckles and short, spiky hair.

The eyes that looked back at Rory now were the same eyes Rory remembered. The ears jutting out from the sides of the narrow head were familiar, too. The rest of the face, however, was foreign to him.

Rory's face was longer than he remembered—long and bony; the cheekbones jutted out. The face still had some freckles, but red bumps of acne overpowered them. Below the acne, bristles of facial hair darkened a hard jawline. And his hair . . . Rory's hair was long, really long. It was still messy, but now the mess was a tangle that fell well past his shoulders—bare and wide but almost skeletal shoulders. Below the shoulders, a thin spray of dark blond hair covered a skinny chest.

Rory knew himself as a seven-year-old kid, but what he was seeing in the mirror was more like a seventeen-year-old teenager. How had he jumped ahead ten years? He suddenly remembered the fairy tale about Rip Van Winkle, who had gone to sleep and slept for twenty years. Had Rory done something like that? But how?

Rory was so freaked out by what was going on that he wanted to run from the bathroom. Turning away from the mirror, Rory shouted again. "Mom!"

His mom didn't answer.

Rory looked down at his bare body. He shivered and looked around wildly, as if the bathroom could help him figure out what had happened to him.

A closer look at the bathroom, however, just made the mystery worse. The bathroom was a mess. The sink, toilet, and tub all had rusty-looking stains, and the tiled floor was scuffed and scummy. Paint peeled from the walls. The bathroom looked like one you'd find in a haunted house. Why?

Whatever was going on, Rory didn't want to face it without clothes. So, Rory threw open the bathroom door and quickly sprinted from the bathroom back into his bedroom. Yanking back the broken closet door, he reached for his clothes.

The clothes, however, weren't what Rory needed. For one thing, they were dirty and wrinkled and worn. For another, they were way, way, way too small. These were the clothes Rory remembered wearing when he was his seven-year-old self. How would they fit this new big version of him?

Rory nearly tore his closet apart trying to find something reasonable to put on. Eventually, he managed to find a pair of black-and-white zebra-striped pajama bottoms that he was able to squirm into. The hems of the legs hit him at knee level, and the waistband was really tight, but he could live with it. It was better than going around without pants on. The only shirt he could find that wasn't so small that it ripped when he tried to put it on was a bright red one. It fit him like it was painted onto his skin, and its hem landed just below his ribs, so his belly was bare. Again, though, it was better than nothing.

The pajamas bottoms and the shirt didn't smell very good. They kind of stank, actually . . . they reeked of old sweat. They were a little stiff, too. But what other choice

DITTOPHOBIA

did Rory have? He wasn't going to wander around without any clothes on!

Without expecting much, Rory looked for socks and shoes that fit. He found socks that he was able to stretch over his feet, but the shoe situation was hopeless. He'd have to stick with socks for now. Maybe if he could find his mom, they could go out and shop for some new clothes.

The paper in the hall was falling off the wall in long, curling strips that drooped onto the wood floor. The floor was thick with dust that was scuffed by large footprints. Rory realized now that those footprints must have been his own. They were the same size as his feet. Had he been walking in his sleep?

The hallway floor was weird, too. It wasn't the wood floor he remembered. Part of the floor was like that floor, but running down the middle of it was a set of metal tracks imbedded in the wood, like streetcar tracks. Rory had seen those once when his parents had taken him to a big city that had cool streetcars that went up and down steep hills. But why were these metal rails in his house? What were they for?

Rory followed the tracks down the hall to the great room and found more of the same decay. The furniture was grimy and all the plush cushions were flattened. There was more peeling wallpaper in here, and the shades that covered the windows were yellowed and limp, as if they could barely manage to cling to their brackets.

Rory looked toward the kitchen. He chewed on his lower lip. There was no way his mom would have let her kitchen get into this state. Not only was it covered in dust, but crumbs were also everywhere. A trail of ants was marching out of the cabinet under the sink. Rory wrinkled his nose. The kitchen smelled awful, too. Was it spoiled food? No, he didn't think so. The air smelled more like the way his grandma's attic had smelled when she'd had a leak in her roof.

The thought of spoiled food made Rory's chest tighten. What if he *had* slept for ten years? Would there be any food left for him?

Rory hurried to the fridge. His feet stirred up dust bunnies as he went. They fluttered over the floor and settled under the edge of the kitchen's lower cabinets.

Marred by too many smudges to count, the refrigerator handle rattled in Rory's grasp as he pulled on it. The fridge door opened, and Rory gawked at its interior. What in the world?

Rory remembered the refrigerator as being filled with plastic shelving and drawers. Juices were on the top shelf. Stuff like ketchup and mustard were on the door. Plastic containers of leftovers were on the middle shelves. Cheese and meats were in the cheese drawer. Veggies and fruits were in two produce drawers at the bottom of the fridge.

That, however, wasn't what Rory was seeing now. The inside of the fridge didn't look like the inside of a fridge. It looked more like a dispenser, with rows of food similar to the ones Rory had seen in vending machines. He leaned forward and looked at the small, yellow wrappers that contained something about the size of a fun-size candy bar. The packages looked old; their edges were a little ratty and the labels had faded. Curious, Rory plucked out one of the packages. He opened it.

DITTOPHOBIA

Without much enthusiasm, Rory lifted a crunchy-looking tan wafer from the packaging. He held it to his nose. It smelled sort of like vanilla, but not really.

Rory's stomach growled. He was hungry, so he figured whatever this was, it was better than going without food. He put the wafer against his tongue. It didn't taste like much, but it didn't taste bad, either. He put the wafer in his mouth and chewed it. Dry and brittle, the wafer disintegrated on his tongue. Rory made a face and managed to swallow the flaky wafer. He quickly went to the sink and turned on the tap.

When clear water ran from the faucet, Rory exhaled in relief. For a second, he'd been afraid that icky water would come out, or worse, no water at all. Rory spotted his glass next to the sink. It looked clean enough, so he grabbed it, filled it, and gulped down half the glass.

When Rory had washed away the dry remains of the wafer, he straightened. What now?

Rory had to find his mom. Maybe she could explain what was going on.

When he reached her door, he called out, "Mom!" She didn't answer, so he tried the door. It was locked.

Rory backed away from the door and frowned at it. The door, he realized, wasn't actually a door. It had no hinge, and there were no gaps around the edges where the door could open away from the wall. Why did his parents' room have a fake door?

Rory turned away from the bizarre imitation door. He could hear the shower running behind the door a few feet farther down the hall, so he moved on and stopped in front of the bathroom door. His mom had to be in the shower. She'd tell him what was going on.

When Rory reached the bathroom door, though, he discovered that it, too, was not a real door. Rory put his ear to the slab of wood that was masquerading as a door. Why was he hearing a shower?

Cocking his head, Rory noticed that the running water sound was not coming from the other side of the fake door as he'd assumed it was. The sound was coming from *above* the "door."

Rory stepped back and looked up. He screwed up his face as he stared at a rectangular black speaker set high on the wall. The "shower" sound came from that speaker.

Rory opened his mouth to call for his mom again, but he abruptly clamped his lips together. If the doors weren't real and the shower wasn't real, was his mom real?

His legs a little shaky and his heart pounding, Rory turned to continue on down the hall. This hall, like the one on the other side of his bedroom, had the same metal tracks set into the wood floor. Rory followed the tracks, and he saw that they split into two sets by his bedroom door. One set of tracks veered toward his room. The other set ran on to the end of the hall. This second set disappeared underneath another door. Was that one real?

Rory ignored the questionable door and followed the metal tracks into his room. There, he saw the tracks continued. They were set into the carpet. Why hadn't he seen that earlier? He'd probably been too baffled by everything else to notice the floor. Now, though, he followed the tracks. They led up to his bed.

Rory scanned the rest of the carpet in his room. Another set of tracks ran from the closet to the bed, and another set ran from the other side of the bed to the doorway leading to the left-side hall.

Rory went around the bed and followed the tracks on the left side of the room out into the hall. There, he turned left and followed another set of tracks to a door at the end of the hall.

Examining the door, Rory decided that this one was real. It had hinges and cracks around the edge of its dirty, white-painted surface. Rory grasped the door's knob and turned it.

At first, the door didn't budge, but Rory was determined to get it open so he took hold of the knob with both hands and yanked.

The door popped open.

Rory jerked back so quickly that he stumbled. His heart began beating fast and hard. Its thrumming filled his ears.

Rory started to turn to run, but before he completed the turn he realized that he wasn't seeing what he thought he was seeing. He had, he suddenly understood, no reason to run.

Rory took a deep breath. He faced what was in the closet.

Looking back at him from the shadows of a small, dusty enclosure, the decrepit purple-blue bunny that was a major player in Rory's ongoing nightmares gazed, dark eyed and still, straight ahead. The bunny was as Rory remembered it from his night terrors. It had tattered fur torn apart so horribly that Rory could see completely through the gaping holes in the bunny's torso. The bunny had deadly looking teeth and claws, but those teeth and claws were rigid and unmoving now.

Rory took a step forward. He leaned in and examined the metal that he could see through the ratty fur.

Rory was so surprised by what he was seeing that he had to clutch the doorframe to keep himself upright. He goggled at what stood before him.

Rory's nightmare creature was nothing more than a spooky life-size figurine. It was a costume hung on a flimsy metallic skeleton. It couldn't move on its own—it was transported into Rory's room on rails. It was just a mechanical trick.

Rory clenched his fists. He slammed the door in the phony creature's face, and he turned to stride back into his room.

There, Rory marched to his closet. He investigated the back of it, and he quickly found the fox version of the creatures that terrorized him at night.

Rory stomped out of the closet and went to his bed. Dropping to his knees, he found a flap in the carpet. Under the carpet was a trapdoor. Beneath the trapdoor, he saw the horrific bear that always blocked his escape from the creatures. It, too, was nothing more than an oversize puppet.

His head starting to pound, Rory left his room via the door on the right and followed that hallway's tracks to the door at the end of the hall. There, he found the disintegrating chick and its cupcake. It was all fake. Every bit of it. But why?

Rory tore through the house to find out what else wasn't real. It didn't take long to discover that the rest of the locked doors weren't actual doors. The only doors that opened were his bedroom doors and the doors that enclosed the nightmare creatures.

Rory walked through the house once more, studying

the dirty floors. He looked for more trapdoors, but he didn't find any.

He returned to the kitchen, unable to let go of a hunch he had about the refrigerator. Although stocked with the dry wafers, the dispenser had to be refilled from somewhere.

Rory flung open the refrigerator door. He glared at the dispenser and its rows of wafers in yellow wrappers. He grabbed the little packages, threw them over his shoulder, and stripped the dispenser completely.

It was attached to the fridge's sides by metal clips. It just took a sharp tug for the dispenser to groan and twang and let go of the clips. Rory fell back and barely kept his balance. Tossing aside the dispenser's guts, he looked into the fridge.

It wasn't actually a fridge.

There was no back to the appliance. Instead, the fridge's interior was a tunnellike enclosure that extended back behind the fridge, reaching through the kitchen's wall. The metal tunnel led to a metal door. Although the door had no handle, Rory could easily see its edges.

Rory hunched over and crawled into the long narrow enclosure. He wriggled forward until he could put his hands on the door. The flimsy metal gave a little under his palms.

Rory lunged forward and shoved the metal, and the door popped loose with a clatter. He clambered forward and looked through the opening. Nothing but blackness looked back at him. But that was better than a pair of glowing eyes.

Not willing to dive headfirst into a space he couldn't

see, Rory backed out of the passage. His mom kept a flashlight in a kitchen drawer, didn't she?

Rory pulled out the drawer, and yes, sure enough, there was a flashlight. Flipping it on, he crawled back into the fridge and shone his light through the opening. Now, in the pale yellow glow of barely there light, Rory could see the bent metal door lying on what looked like a concrete floor. The floor looked like it was just a few feet below the opening.

Rory could see now, but he couldn't see very much, so again he backed out and this time reentered the passage feetfirst. Scooting on his butt, he squirmed forward until he could stick his feet through the opening at the back of the dispenser.

Rory landed in a crouch with one foot on concrete and the other foot on the fallen metal door. He straightened and quickly turned in a circle, shining his flashlight beam out around him.

Rory frowned. What was this place?

Rory was in a concrete corridor. In the faint glow of his flashlight, it was hard to see the details of what was around him. The corridor, however, appeared to be lined with metal racks. The racks were filled with, of all things, something that looked like scuba tanks.

Rory stepped over to one. He aimed his light at some writing on it: DANGER. COMPRESSED GAS.

Gas? What kind of gas?

Rory leaned over and sniffed the valve. He could smell nothing but the corridor's damp.

Rory looked around some more. All the tanks, he realized, were connected to rubber hoses. The network of hoses lined the hallway, and they all came together in

DITTOPHOBIA

a cluster that fed into the wall next to the opening Rory had just come through.

Whatever the gas was, it was being pumped into Rory's house.

Rory scrunched up his face and walked down the corridor, his flashlight's rays zipping this way and that. The tangle of black hoses that wormed all over the walls reminded Rory of snakes, and even though the hoses weren't moving, Rory kept his gaze on them as he stepped carefully past the gas tanks. This attention to the hoses was what led him to an old gray machine at the end of the corridor.

Rory didn't know anything about machines, but he could tell this one wasn't running. It had a fan sort of like the purple one in his room, and the fan's blades were still. No sound came from the machine. Rory went on past it.

A few feet beyond the machine, just before an open doorway, Rory came to a small, gray metal desk. Rory aimed his light at the desk's surface, and the beam illuminated the metal part of a clipboard lying at one end of the desk. Rory could see the edges of some curling papers clamped onto the clipboard. Maybe something on the papers would explain what was going on.

Rory picked up the clipboard. He moved his light so it shone directly on it.

The first thing Rory saw on the top sheet of paper was a date. It was a date just a month after his seventh birthday. He read a handwritten entry next to the date.

"Subject continues to react with fear," Rory read aloud, "to what he perceives to be creatures. Fear level: nine."

"Perceives to be," Rory repeated.

Rory pursed his lips.

Rory wasn't the best reader in the world. He'd struggled with reading in school, but his friend, Wade, was a really good reader. He'd taught Rory lots of words. So, Rory knew what *perceives* meant. It meant that his brain was telling him something, and given the way the entry on the clipboard was worded, Rory concluded that whatever his brain was telling him wasn't necessarily the truth.

Rory read as fast as he could. He flipped through the pages on the clipboard. Because most of the entries were short, and nearly all of them were the same or similar, it didn't take Rory long to figure out what he was looking at.

When Rory reached the bottom page on the clipboard, he flipped back to the top one. He looked at the date again.

Rory dropped the clipboard and began searching the rest of the desktop and the desk's drawers. He didn't find any other papers.

A straight-backed, black metal chair sat in front of the desk. Rory, too shocked to continue standing, dropped onto it. He stared at the clipboard. Then he turned and aimed his light back down the corridor at the rows of gas tanks. Finally, he shifted the light to the machine that wasn't running.

Tears filled Rory's eyes. At the same time, his face heated up. He clenched his teeth.

It was all fake. Everything he'd thought he knew about his life was a lie.

Did I ever have the life I thought I was living? Rory wondered.

Although his memories were fuzzy, Rory had clear images in his head of his mom and his dad. He could

DITTOPHOBIA

remember talking with them and doing things with them. The same was true of school and his friend, Wade. In Rory's mind, the house he'd woke up in that morning was his house (although the house in his memories was clean and new and tidy). But none of the images in Rory's head were real. Nothing in Rory's life was real.

According to the papers on the clipboard, the gas in the gas tanks were hallucinogens. These were drugs that made him think he was seeing and doing things he wasn't seeing and doing. The gas was what made him think he was living in the house with his parents. The gas made him think he had to go to school. The gas made him think he was eating real food when in fact the whole time he was eating the awful wafers. (The wafers, the papers said, were freeze-dried sources of all the nutrients a human body needed. That might have been true, Rory thought, but given how skinny he was, he didn't think the wafers were enough for him anymore.)

The gas was also the source of his night terrors. Apparently, the whole thing was a nasty experiment designed to study the effects of ongoing fear in children. Whoever was behind the experiment wanted to see what happened if a child faced the same horrors night after night after night with no real life during the day to balance the awfulness of the nightmares.

Because the latest entry on the clipboard had been made the same year that Rory had turned seven, he concluded that this awful place had been abandoned ten years before. The gas lines and the food dispenser and everything else must have been automated.

Rory looked again at the silent machine. He wasn't sure, but he thought the machine was a pump. If it was, it was responsible for the stream of gas that kept Rory living in an illusion. It must have broken down. That was why the gas stopped. And when the gas stopped, Rory saw through the illusion. That was why he could now see that he was a teenager instead of the boy he'd thought he was.

No wonder none of Rory's clothes fit. No wonder the house was a mess. Suddenly, it all made sense.

Rory hadn't been sleeping for the last ten years; he'd been up and conscious. Everything he'd done, though, he'd done in a haze caused by the gas that constantly hissed into the house through the vents in the ceiling. That gas had kept him from seeing what was really going on around him. It had kept him locked in a perpetual childhood, understanding his surroundings on only the most basic level. That gas had kept Rory in a jail of misery.

The whole experiment was mean. Really, really mean. Someone had been here watching Rory, recording all his reactions. And now, it was even worse. For ten years, the experiment had been running on its own. There wasn't even a watcher anymore. No one was here to make sure everything worked right. No one made sure Rory was cared for.

He returned his attention to the machine. What if it restarted?

Rory jumped up. He had to make sure the gas wouldn't start to flow again.

Because Rory didn't know how to do anything with the machine, he figured the best thing for him to do was make sure the machine wasn't connected to anything. If it wasn't hooked up to a hose, it couldn't move the gas. *That makes sense*, he thought.

Rory hurried over to the machine. Without much trouble, he found where a giant black rubber hose was clamped to one side of the machine. The mega hose led to the smaller ones that snaked across the walls and led to all the gas tanks. This giant hose had to be the one that moved the gas through a system that fed into the house.

Rory peered at the clamp. A screw held the clamp in place. Scanning the area around the machine, Rory spotted an open, scarred, green-metal toolbox. Rummaging in it, he came up with a screwdriver. Awkwardly, because he wasn't yet used to having such large hands, Rory managed to unscrew the clamp. He removed it and pulled the black hose away from the machine. It came loose with a squelching snick.

Okay. If Rory was right about the machine, it couldn't move the gas even if it started again.

What now? Rory asked himself.

The answer to that question was easy. Rory had to get out of this place. If he could get out, he could find someone who could help him find his real home . . . if he actually had one. Well, even if he didn't have a home, anyplace had to be better than where he was.

Rory pointed his light through a narrow doorway just beyond the metal desk. That was his only option now so he stepped through it and found himself in another corridor. Although this one wasn't lined with gas tanks or rubber hoses, it still had "snakes" running all over the walls. These snakes were made of metal, and they looked like electrical lines or maybe water pipes. Rory really couldn't tell.

This corridor was dirtier than the last one. The corridor's pale gray walls were covered with streaks of grease, and the lines and pipes had woolly layers of dust. It smelled like a mechanic's shop. Rory could remember being in one when he'd gone with his dad to take the family van to the shop.

Or did he really remember that?

Rory shook off the question and kept going.

As Rory picked his way through the corridor, he was nervous and jumpy, but he wasn't out-and-out frightened. He guessed the reason he wasn't in total panic mode was because he felt more determined than scared. Yeah, exploring a dark and creepy place by himself wasn't any fun, but Rory knew it had to be done.

He was angry, and that anger was keeping him going. He didn't think he'd find any people, either. Obviously, whoever had worked here, watching Rory be scared all the time, was no longer here.

He wished they were. He'd like to give them a piece of his mind.

When the corridor that Rory was in connected up with another one that led both left and right, Rory shrugged and went right. One direction was as good as any other at this point. Rory had no way of knowing where he'd find a way out.

Because the concrete place had no windows, Rory couldn't tell how much time passed as he explored. Time lost its meaning as he moved along, his head turning left and right constantly.

Okay, so maybe he was a little more scared than he wanted to admit.

The rooms were disturbing. One was obviously some kind of observation station. It had slanted glass walls that looked out at a darkness Rory couldn't see into. Above one of the glass walls, there was a panel of unlit colored lights. Even though the lights weren't on, Rory could see that the four lights were different colors—one blue, one green, one pink, and one yellow. On an adjacent glass wall, a poster of a wild-looking girl with red pigtails had the word CELEBRATE printed across the top. A darkened control panel was under the glass wall with the lights. A row of upright gas tanks lined the wall to the right of it. A series of fans were on the wall on the other side of it.

What was beyond the glass walls? Suddenly afraid of what might have been lurking in that darkness, Rory ducked down below the level of the glass. He tried to reassure himself as he crouched there. It was probably just the setting of some other mean experiment. He flicked his flashlight beam toward the poster again. The pigtailed girl's wide-mouthed grin was much too toothy to be friendly. Rory quickly walked out of the room and moved on.

Not long after he found the observation room, Rory entered a room that looked like a big dance floor with a stage. On the stage, a metal ballerina was frozen in place with her arms above her head. She wore a purple metal skirt, the stiff kind that stuck out from her waist.

Why is this here? Rory wondered as he stared at the ballerina.

He shone his light around and didn't see any kind of control panel or observation booth. He did, however, see a doorway on the far side of the dance floor. Was it an exit? His way out?

Rory practically ran across the big dance floor. He moved so quickly that dust swirled up around his sock-covered feet as they slapped against the dirty black-and-white-tiled floor.

The doorway led to yet another corridor, with yet another open door at the end. Maybe that was the way out.

Maybe it wasn't.

Stepping through the open door, Rory found himself in a room crawling with more electrical wall snakes. They were the big metal cords that held bunches of smaller cords inside them. All the cords led into and out of a large metal box.

A breaker box, Rory thought.

His dad had—maybe—taught him about the breaker box in their house. Rory knew how to open the box and flip the switches to turn lights back on if they went out. Would it work in here? Would turning on more lights help him find his way out?

Rory picked his way past the tangle of electrical lines. *Is it safe in here?* he wondered.

He wasn't sure he cared. After everything he'd been put through, he just wanted to get out—at any cost.

Rory opened the metal box and began flipping rows of switches. He shifted them all from the left to the right. Nothing happened.

Rory turned away from the box and flicked off his flashlight to see if any light had come on. He quickly turned his flashlight on again. Flipping the switches hadn't changed the surrounding darkness. Rory left the room.

In the corridor, Rory didn't see any changes resulting from the switches he'd flipped. He sighed and turned left out of the electrical room. Walking forward, Rory

DITTOPHOBIA

discovered that the corridor dead-ended not too far past the big dance room, but another corridor jutted off to the right. Rory headed down it.

Rory passed another right turn. This time, though, the corridor he was in continued. He decided to go to its end before he came back to check out the right turn.

Rory followed the corridor until it took a hard right a little farther along. There, he found himself in another corridor that led to two open doorways. Checking the one on the left first, he discovered a room filled with what looked like animatronic parts. Metal arms and legs and heads and torsos were stacked on shelves along with tangles of wires and mounds of gears. Rory thought the dusty metal tables near the shelves looked like tables in doctors' offices. He didn't like doctors' offices. Probably. If his memories were real, that is. He left the room and went into the room on the opposite side of the corridor.

The really big room across from the one filled with robotic parts looked like a place where people went to eat and watch shows. The room had a big stage on one end and rows of purple-cloth-covered tables stretching out from the stage. The tables sat on thin, old carpet. Even in his flashlight's minimal light, Rory could see that the carpet was purple with a gold star pattern.

Even with the flashlight, it was difficult to see much else in the high-ceilinged room, but Rory spotted a faded sign over the stage that read FUNTIME AUDITORIUM. Deflated balloons were scattered over the tables and the carpeted floor.

In the shadows of a corner not far from the doorway leading out of the room, the cracked and dusty shell of an animatronic pirate fox lay crumpled against the wall. When he spotted it, Rory let out a little yelp. The fox looked a lot like Rory's nightmare fox. This fox, though, wasn't as torn up as the nightmare fox. The black eyes were unfocused, but Rory still avoided looking at them. He hurried out of the auditorium, fighting the urge to shut the door behind him for safety's sake.

Of course there were more animatronics. The repair room suggested there were many. He shouldn't be so scared of this one.

Even though this fox had haunted his nightmares for ten years at least.

Finding himself in yet another corridor, Rory looked left and right and tried to remember the layout of what he'd seen so far. If he went right, he'd come back to the corridor that had led away from the electrical room. He decided to go back to that corridor and retrace his steps to the hall he'd passed, the one that had led off to the right.

Rory got to that corridor quickly, and his exploration was even faster. That corridor was short, and it led directly into another room. This room, Rory decided, had to be the heart of the whole place he was in. It looked to be a control room.

Like the room that had the circus-looking lights, this room was walled on two sides by slanted glass. This was obviously another observation station. He didn't know what had been observed, and he didn't care. He didn't care about the big, currently nonfunctioning fan on the end wall between the glass walls, either. The weird clown faces on the wall near the fan and the puppet masks on stands atop two cabinets of metal drawers under the fan

DITTOPHOBIA

didn't interest him, either. He thought the clowns were super eerie, but they were just plastic faces.

What got Rory's attention as soon as he entered the room were the metal drawers. There were six of them, three in each of the two cabinets that flanked the massive fan. Rory rushed over to the cabinets. Maybe he'd find something in the drawers to help him get the heck out of here.

For the next several minutes, Rory yanked open drawers and pawed through jangles of tools and masses of paper. At first, he didn't find anything helpful. In the fourth drawer, though, he found blueprints to what was labeled UNDERGROUND TESTING FACILITY.

So that's where he was! He was underground!

Even the sunshine in Rory's house hadn't been real. No wonder he'd never been able to raise the shades and look outside.

Rory spread out the blueprints and leaned over them. Because Rory's mom was an interior designer (or at least he thought she was), Rory had seen architectural blueprints before. He wasn't great at picking out all their details, but he could get the general layout of a place from them. Rory studied these, and he quickly found what he was looking for: a way out.

Beyond this control room, down a short hallway, there was an elevator. That had to lead back up to the real world.

Excited, Rory trotted out of the control room and weaved his way around it to find the little corridor that led to the elevator. In minutes, he reached a circular metal room with a grated floor and a massive ceiling fan overhead. The ceiling fan wasn't moving, and the range of Rory's flashlight wasn't long enough for Rory to see what was under the grated floor. But what he could see, straight ahead of him, was a set of big, smooth stainless-steel elevator doors.

Rory rushed forward. As he did, he noticed that this room didn't have the musty smell that the rest of the corridors and rooms had. It smelled fresher. *That was a good sign*, he thought.

Going deeper into the room, Rory passed another network of metal electrical lines and two posters. One poster had the image of the red-pigtailed girl that Rory had seen before and the other had an image of the ballerina he'd found on the stage in the big dance room. Rory barely glanced at the posters. He zeroed in on a small, square control panel to the right of the elevator. Above a keypad, a big red button promised his freedom.

Rory reached the button. His fingers tingling in anticipation, he pushed it.

Nothing happened.

Rory stared at the elevator doors. Was it one of those silent elevators? Could it have been working and he just didn't hear it?

Rory waited. His heart rate picked up. His palms began to sweat.

He waited some more.

Still, nothing happened.

Rory hit the red button again. It didn't even click.

Leaning toward the control panel, Rory randomly punched buttons. He did this for a full minute. Yet again, nothing happened.

Rory exhaled heavily. He shone his light into the darkness.

DITTOPHOBIA

Oh right. Of course the elevator didn't work. No lights. No power.

Rory groaned in disappointment. He'd been sure he'd found the way out.

How could he get the elevator working?

Rory pounded on the red button, but he knew he was acting like the seven-year-old he hadn't been for ten years. He turned away from the button. He had to find a way to get the elevator working. But how?

The only thing Rory could think to do was go back to the control room. He hadn't gone through the last two drawers after he'd found the blueprints. Maybe something in there would help him.

Giving the elevator one last longing glance, Rory left the room and headed back to the control room. His plan was a long shot, but he didn't know what else to do.

The fifth drawer Rory went through was no help. The sixth drawer, though, gave Rory some new hope. In that drawer, he found a small battery-powered two-way radio.

"All right!" Rory exclaimed when he spotted the gray metal radio. He knew how to use one of these. He and his friend, Wade, had used walkie-talkies a lot.

Or in Rory's memory, they had. Were his memories real? Was *Wade* real?

At this point, Rory figured he didn't need to know what was real and what wasn't. All he needed to do was get the radio working. If the batteries were still good (*please, please be good*, he silently begged), he could at least try to reach Wade. If Wade was real, maybe he'd still have his radio. If he wasn't, maybe someone else would answer Rory.

Rory leaned over the radio and toggled the "on" switch. Static spurted out into the room.

"Yes!" Rory pumped his fist. The radio worked!

Dropping to the grated floor, Rory set the radio in his lap. He fiddled with the frequency dial and then he keyed the mic. "Rory to Wade. Come in, Wade. Over," he said into the mic.

Static crackled.

Rory tried again. "Wade, this is Rory. Do you read? Over."

More static. Then Rory heard a couple blurps of garbled voices. After another ear-jabbing stream of crackling, Rory heard what sounded like "Roar are there."

Rory tweaked the radio's settings. "This is Rory? Who's there? Over."

The radio spit a couple of buzzing sounds, then Rory was able to hear a voice clearly. "Rory! Is that you? Really?"

"Wade?"

"Yeah, dude," Wade shouted. "Where are you?"

"You're real?" Rory asked.

"Huh?" Wade's laugh came through the radio's speaker. "Sure, I'm real. How about you? It's been *ten years*! Where've you been?"

Rory clutched the mic so hard that the plastic dug into his palm. Where should he start?

Before Rory could even try to explain what had happened to him, Wade started talking again. "I'm glad I kept this old walkie," Wade said. "I was going to toss it a few years ago when Dad got me a new radio, but I guess I'm sentimental or something. I couldn't bring myself to throw it away. It reminded me of you, and getting rid of it felt like I'd be throwing away our friendship. I never expected to ever use the thing again, though! I never, ever thought I'd hear your voice coming through it! That's for sure." Wade's whoop came through the radio's speaker. "Your mom and dad are going to flip out when they find out you're alive. They were so desperate to find you, man. The police gave up the search after just a year, but your parents didn't. They hired all kinds of private detectives, and they had a website and everything."

"Had?" Rory repeated.

Wade's sigh came through the walkie-talkie's speaker. "It's been so long, dude. But they never stopped missing you."

Rory's eyes moistened. He really did have a mom and dad who cared about him.

"I miss them, too," Rory said. "And you, Wade."

"Fido misses you, too," Wade said. "Your parents kept your room the way it always was, and Fido goes in the room every day and sniffs around. That's what your mom told me the last time I talked to her."

Fido! Rory had forgotten all about Fido. He had a dog. Fido was a spaniel mix with long, silky ears. How could Rory have forgotten about Fido? Rory had been four years old when they'd gotten Fido as a puppy. That meant the dog was thirteen now.

"Fido's an old dude now," Wade said as if reading Rory's mind, "but he still gets around okay."

Rory felt tears running down his cheeks. He wiped them away.

"You have a little sister now, too," Wade said. He chuckled. "Well, not so little now. She's nine."

A sister? Rory thought. *What would it be like to have a sister?*

"When are you coming home?" Wade asked. "We'll have a big party. You can meet my girlfriend."

"Girlfriend?"

Wade's laugh came through the radio's speaker again. "Yeah. I know we never let girls into our clubhouse, but things change."

Not for me, Rory thought. "Is our clubhouse still there?" Rory asked.

"Sure is," Wade said. "I kept that up, too. I couldn't stand the idea of it getting torn down . . . just in case. Even the tire swing is still there."

"I can't wait to see it again," Rory said.

"We'll have a party in the clubhouse, too," Wade said.

"I have so much to catch up on," Rory said. "I haven't been in school all these years. I'm as dumb as a bagel." Rory remembered that Wade had always told him that bagels were a "dumb breakfast food."

Wade laughed loudly. "That's pretty dumb," he said. He must have remembered their banter about what was good for breakfast.

"I can't wait to see you again," Rory said. "And Mom and Dad and Fido. And my room and my yard. And I can't wait to meet my sister."

Rory's head was filling with images of everything he'd forgotten he had and things he didn't even know he had. He could see himself pushing his sister on the tire swing. Maybe he'd even let her in the clubhouse.

"Me neither," Wade said. "So, when can you get here?"

Rory sighed. He had to tell Wade what was going on.

"I don't know where I am, Wade," he said.

"What do you mean? Has someone been holding you prisoner? Are you okay?"

Rory looked at the bony hand that held the radio mic. No, he wasn't exactly okay.

"I'm okay enough, I guess," Rory said. "I'm in an underground place. The blueprints I found said it's a testing facility. There's no one here but me now. I've been in a fake house that's been filled with a gas that made me see things that weren't there. It's all been a big experiment. Whoever set this up has been scaring me every night with terrifying nightmares."

"That's awful, dude!" Wade said. "Where are the people now, the ones who set it all up?"

"I don't know," Rory said. "The gas stopped this morning, and that's the only reason I found out that what I thought was real isn't. The last thing I remember was that I was still seven years old. It totally weirded me out this morning when I saw the way I look now."

"Whoa," Wade said. "That's heavy. I can't even imagine."

Wade stopped speaking, and his mic clicked. Faint static filled the silence that followed his words. Rory wasn't sure what to say next.

"Can you see anything at all that might give you a clue about where you are?" Wade asked.

"No. Nothing," Rory said. "I'm in a concrete underground place. I've looked everywhere, and nothing I've found tells me where it is."

"You have to get out of there," Wade said.

Rory wanted to say "duh," but he thought that would be rude. Instead, he said, "I've been trying to find a way out. So far, no luck."

"Tell me again about what you've found," Wade said.

For the next several minutes, Rory gave Wade a detailed description of the house and the concrete corridors and rooms in the testing facility. Finally, he asked, "Can you think of anything I missed?"

Wade was silent for a few seconds. Then his mic clicked. "I think the key to escaping is going to be in that fake house," Wade said. "You said it has power, right?"

"Yeah," Rory said.

"Okay," Wade said. "If the rest of the facility doesn't have power, there must be some kind of generator keeping that house going. If you can find the generator and disconnect it and then get it back into the facility, you might be able to power everything back up, including the elevator."

Rory sat up straight. That wasn't a bad idea. "That's brilliant," he said.

"I just hope it works," Wade said.

"Me too," Rory said.

"Too bad they can't trace these old radios," Wade said. "If you had a cell phone, we could trace you."

"They can do that now?" Rory asked.

"They can do all kinds of stuff," Wade said. "As soon as we stop talking, I'll call the police and tell them everything you told me. Maybe they can figure out a way to find you."

Rory felt a little shiver of excitement at that idea. Then the excitement fizzled. How in the world could the police find an underground facility when they didn't even have a clue about where to look?

No, Rory was going to have to get himself out of here.

"I'll do what you suggested," Rory said, "just in case the police can't help."

"Good idea."

For several seconds, they were both quiet. Then Wade said, "I wish there was something else I could do for you."

Rory did, too, but he said, "You've done a lot. Just by being there. And by giving me an idea of what to do." He took a breath and squeezed the mic. "Now, I'd better go do it. I don't know how long I've been wandering around the facility. At night, fake night that is, the house gets . . ." Rory stopped. He was thinking about the nightmare creatures. Shaking off a shiver, he said, "I need to find the generator soon."

"Yeah, you'd better get going," Wade said.

"Okay," Rory said.

"Let me know how it goes," Wade said. "I'll be here."

"Thanks. I will."

They said awkward good-byes. Rory turned off the radio.

Rory had kept his fear in control when he'd been in the concrete corridors, but as soon as he crawled back into the fake house, his fear turned big and ugly and made him want to curl up in a ball and cry. The great room shades were dark. Real or not, the sun was down. What time was it? Rory wasn't sure. It might be close to midnight. That's when the hidden creatures were going to come to life. Rory needed to find the generator and get out of the house before that happened.

Even though it made no sense, Rory was still terrified of the creatures. Knowing they were nothing but motorized mannequins didn't take away his terror. He guessed that after so many years, the dread was too much a part of him to go away that quickly.

Rory stood next to the kitchen island and thought hard. The refrigerator hummed softly as he tried to figure out how to go about finding the generator. The hum helped him think; he liked the steady purr. Without that sound, the house would have been way, way too silent. Rory didn't like silence. Too much silence reminded him of how alone he was. When he thought about how alone he was, he couldn't think about anything else.

"Come on," he urged himself. "Figure it out."

Rory had already searched the whole house, and he hadn't seen a generator. Where hadn't he looked?

Rory thought about the creatures in the closets at the end of the halls. When he'd found them, he hadn't gotten too close to them. Could a generator be tucked behind the monster bunny or the monster chick?

Rory shuddered. He really didn't want to go look behind the creatures that had tortured him through so many long, miserable nights, but he had to do it.

Straightening his shoulders, Rory left the kitchen and headed down the right hall. *I can do this*, he told himself as he walked toward the closed door at the end of the hall.

"They're just machines," Rory said out loud when he was just a few feet from the door.

That's when the closet door opened.

The click of the door unlatching was loud in the silent house. It froze Rory in place.

His heart leaping up into his mouth, Rory watched the closet door swing out, opening farther and farther and farther. Rory's gaze was latched on to the door, but his attention shifted when he saw movement beyond the door.

DITTOPHOBIA

Rory clenched his fists. A grinding whir filled the hallway, and the ratty yellow chick-like creature began moving. Rory's nightmare was coming to life!

Rory's throat tightened. His legs suddenly felt rubbery, and he shifted his feet to keep his balance.

When his feet moved, Rory felt the hard metal of the railing in the floor. He looked down.

"It's just a mechanical monster," he said aloud.

Lifting his gaze, Rory looked ahead at the holey yellow chick. "You're not real," he said to it.

The chick didn't reply, of course. It couldn't. It was a machine.

Feeling stronger now, Rory widened his stance and faced the chick—up close, he could see how fake it really was—as it glided out of the closet and down the hall toward Rory. Rory once again shifted his gaze to the floor. He could clearly see that the chick's feet were attached to rollers that skimmed along on the railing set into the floor.

"You can't hurt me," Rory said to the chick.

Again, the chick did nothing but what its machine programming told it to do. It rolled forward along the railing until the railing curved toward Rory's bedroom door. The chick's metal feet clanked against the railing, and the chick disappeared into Rory's bedroom.

Rory rubbed his arms. Even though he'd now seen the machinery working, he still felt nervous being so near to one of the creatures from his nightmares.

"Just get on with it," Rory told himself.

Rushing forward, Rory checked out the now-empty closet to see if it held a generator. It didn't.

★ ★ ★

Back in the kitchen, Rory looked around. He'd checked out the other creature closet, too; the one on the end of the left hallway. By the time he did, purple-blue bunny had rolled into his room. The bunny's closet wasn't hiding a generator, either.

Where else could Rory look?

When Rory's gaze landed on the island's cabinet, he realized that he couldn't remember ever opening it. He turned and looked around the rest of the kitchen. Had he ever gotten anything out of any of the cabinets? He'd opened the one drawer to get the flashlight, but he couldn't remember opening anything else.

Rory looked over at the sink. His small glass sat there near the tap. That was the only glass he could ever remember using. He never used plates, and he always got his food from the fridge. What if . . .?

Rory looked down. The largest cabinet in the kitchen was the one in front of him. Was it big enough to hide a generator? Rory dropped to his knees. The floor felt gritty beneath his bare skin, and dust puffed up around him as he scooted closer to the cabinet.

Could it be that easy? he asked himself.

Rory grasped the cabinet's gray handles. He pulled the cabinet doors open. And his heart sank. No generator.

The only thing behind the cabinets was thick gray rubber. The rubber's surface was uneven; it reminded Rory of waffles.

Rory started to stand so he could check the other cabinets, but he paused and cocked his head. His ears were telling him something. What was it?

DITTOPHOBIA

Rory held his breath and listened. All he could hear was the refrigerator's hum. Why was that important?

Turning to look at the fridge, Rory wondered if the generator was in the fridge, maybe in the part that was supposed to be a freezer. He once again started to stand, but as soon as he did, he realized what his ears were telling him.

The rumbling purr that he'd thought was the fridge wasn't actually coming from the fridge. Why had he never noticed that before?

It made sense, now that he thought about it. The fridge wasn't a real fridge. The inside of it was just a dispenser. It wasn't cold. So why would it need a motor?

No, the motor Rory could hear wasn't in the fridge.

Rory leaned forward, toward the lumpy gray rubber. He sucked in a quick breath of surprise. The motor sound was coming from behind the rubber.

Rory reached out and put his palms against the rubber. He began running his hands over it, searching for a seam or something he could grab onto.

It took only seconds for Rory's fingers to slip into a slight gap between some of the waffle-like dimples in the rubber. He dug the tips of his fingers farther into the gap so he could grip the rubber. Once he had a good hold on it, he pulled it toward him.

At first, the rubber didn't give, but when Rory leaned away from the island, yanking hard, the rubber made a squishy crunching sound and tore loose. Immediately, the growl of an engine filled the kitchen. Rory fell back on his butt, a big chunk of gray rubber clutched in his fists.

Tossing aside the rubber, Rory looked into the island cabinet... right at a faded orange generator. The generator was vibrating. It was chugging along steadily.

Rory looked at the rubber. It was soundproofing, he realized. The rubber had muffled the generator's motor, and for some reason it had made it seem like the sound was coming from the fridge. Or maybe it was the hallucinogenic gas that had done that. Rory had misinterpreted everything about his life for years and years. It wasn't a surprise that he'd never pinpointed the motor sound during that time.

Rory immediately shifted back to his knees and studied the droning machine. The generator wasn't big—maybe three feet by two and a half feet. It was probably heavy, though. Rory reached for its metal frame and started to tug on it.

Yes, it was heavy. Very heavy. It didn't budge.

Rory, however, was determined. He repositioned his knees and got a better grip on the frame. He started to pull on it again. This time, letting out a metallic groan, the generator scooted forward a couple inches.

"Hello, Rory."

Rory snatched his hands back from the generator frame and dropped his head back to look up at the ceiling. The voice he'd just heard had come from above him.

Was someone here, after all? Was someone watching him?

"Please don't disrupt the generator, Rory," the voice said.

Rory immediately spotted a large white speaker on the ceiling above him. Tucked between two gray metal light fixtures, the speaker blended right into the white-painted

DITTOPHOBIA

ceiling. That must have been why Rory had never seen it before . . . that and the fact that the gas he'd been inhaling had been making him see things that weren't there and not see things that were there.

"Who are you?" Rory asked the voice.

"The generator is what keeps everything running, Rory," the voice said. "It's taking care of you."

The voice coming from the speaker was a man's voice, maybe a man about Rory's dad's age. It was a very nice voice. The voice was low and smooth. It was calm and soothing.

"Who are you?" Rory asked again.

"You know you want to be here, Rory," the voice said, "and the generator makes it possible for you to stay here. It's hooked up to a steady supply of gas, Rory. Always there for you."

"Why can't I see you?" Rory asked.

If someone was here, Rory wanted to see them face-to-face. Why would the man talking to him stay hidden? Why didn't the man come out to talk to him when Rory was wandering through all the concrete corridors? Why didn't the man ever spend time with Rory?

"You ran away from home," the voice said. "Don't you remember?"

Rory pushed his hair out of his face as he concentrated on what the voice was saying. *I ran away?* he thought.

"You didn't fit in at school, Rory," the voice said.

Rory's questions suddenly didn't feel important. Even though Rory couldn't see who was speaking, the sound of the voice felt like a warm hug. He closed his eyes, and in his mind he could see a reassuring smile.

"You had so much trouble in class, Rory," the voice said. "You couldn't understand the equations in math. You had trouble with your reading."

Rory frowned. Yes, he remembered that now. He hated school. He felt stupid when he was at school. He felt like he was wrong somehow, like he couldn't get anything right. He felt like an outcast at school. Wade was his only friend.

"And the girls, Rory," the voice continued. "Remember how the girls thought you were wimpy?"

Rory hunched his shoulders. He remembered that now, too. That was why he and Wade had built their clubhouse. Girls didn't like Wade, either. So, they'd built a place where girls weren't allowed. Not that any girls wanted to be there, but the small wood sign that had NO GIRLS etched onto its surface made Rory and Wade feel like it was their *choice* not to have girls around.

"You came here because you knew you'd be taken care of here," the voice said. "You *have* been taken care of here. Here, you're never an outcast. You're never wrong. You've been watched over and cared for. That was something your parents never did, Rory. Remember?"

Rory bunched up his fists. Yes, he remembered. All his parents ever did was work. His dad was never home. His mom was gone most of the time, too, and when she was home, all she ever did was tell him how wrong he was. *Don't leave smudges, Rory. Pick up your clothes, Rory. Make your bed, Rory. Comb your hair, Rory. It's a mess.* Rory's mom cared more about how things looked than she did about her own son.

"You're safe here, Rory," the voice said. "This is your home. You've been watched over here. You've never been

DITTOPHOBIA

abandoned. Never left alone. All these years, you've been cared for. Because you're special, Rory, and you deserve to live in this special place. Safe and secure. Never alone. This is your home."

Rory hugged himself and started rocking back and forth. He stared at the generator.

Rory thought about talking to Wade over the radio. He thought about what Wade had said. Wade had said Rory's parents missed him. That had made Rory feel good. Rory really loved the idea of going home and seeing his room and the clubhouse. He wanted to pet Fido and meet his sister.

Rory stiffened. What if his sister didn't like him? Why would she? No one besides Wade had liked Rory when he was little. That was the whole reason he'd run away to begin with. He'd never been able to be what people wanted him to be. He'd always come up short. He never did anything the way anyone wanted . . . not his parents, not his teachers, and not the other kids in his class. Why would it be any different now?

Rory had hated feeling so left out. He'd always felt so *wrong*. He hated the feeling of being made fun of. He hated feeling stupid.

Did Rory really want to go back to a world where he didn't fit in? It had been ten years. He hadn't learned anything in that time. He'd be so far behind. He'd be even more of an outcast than he'd been before. All he'd ever do was let people down. All he'd ever be was lonely.

Rory's eyes welled up, and tears began streaming down his face. No, Rory couldn't go home. This place, no matter how fake, was now the only home where he fit in.

Letting his tears flow, Rory reached out and picked up the gray, waffled rubber. He reset the rubber against the front of the generator, pressing hard to be sure it stayed. Then he closed the island cabinet door.

Rory sniffled and stood. Pushing aside the images of an outside world that he now knew he could never return to, Rory turned and faced the refrigerator.

Wiping his face, Rory took a deep breath. Then he crawled back through the vent-like tunnel that led out behind the fridge. Dropping to the concrete floor of the rubber-hose-lined corridor, he walked past all the gas tanks until he reached the old gray machine.

Stiffly, Rory reached into the toolbox and found the screwdriver he'd used to unclamp the main hose that led from the machine. Rory faced the machine, refit the hose, and screwed the clamp tight again. He stepped back and studied the machine.

When he'd looked at the machine before, Rory hadn't had a clue as to why it had stopped running, but now, he could easily see that its power cord was loose. Rory pushed the cord back into its socket, and the machine roared to life. Settling into a buzzing hum, the machine vibrated, and the rubber hose that connected to all the gas tanks flexed and went rigid. The gas was flowing again.

Rory wormed his way back through the metal door at the rear of the fake fridge. He squirmed forward until he could put his feet on the kitchen floor. Once he was upright, he bent over and picked up the discarded wafer dispenser. Then he turned to clamp it back into place. He replaced all the faded yellow packets. As he lined them up, he realized how tired he was. He was so drowsy. He could barely keep his eyes open.

Closing the refrigerator door, Rory rubbed his forehead. Why was he standing in front of the fridge? It was late.

Rory turned and looked at the dark window shades in the great room. It was *really* late. He should be in bed.

Rory's gaze landed on his red backpack. He frowned. Hadn't he gone to school today? He chewed on the inside of his cheek. He couldn't remember.

Rory sighed and shrugged. It didn't matter. What mattered was that he needed to get in bed.

Rory left the great room and started scampering down the long left-side hall, eager to get to his room. His hand trailed along the curved wood chair rail as he went.

Pausing by the bathroom door, Rory canted his head and tried to remember whether he'd brushed his teeth already. He was pretty sure he had. So why had he been in the kitchen?

Rory shrugged again. Whatever. He was so tired. He just wanted to be in bed.

Rory trotted into his bedroom and shut the door behind him. Crossing to the other door on the right side of the room, he closed it, too. Then he made sure his closet doors were closed.

Rory yawned loudly and turned to look at his nice, cushy quilt. It looked so fresh and clean and inviting.

Rory dashed to his bed and dove under his covers. Glancing at his red alarm clock, Rory saw that it was well after midnight.

Knowing it was so late made Rory shiver, so he

snuggled down into his nice warm bed. Pulling his quilt up over his head, he closed his eyes.

At the end of the concrete corridor filled with gas tanks, the gas pump rumbled steadily. In the ceiling above the pump, behind a metal grate, a tape recorder clicked. It then whirred loudly—the sound of a cassette rewinding.

Another click.

The cassette was once again ready . . . for the next time Rory wandered too far.

ABOUT THE AUTHORS

Scott Cawthon is the author of the bestselling video game series *Five Nights at Freddy's*, and while he is a game designer by trade, he is first and foremost a storyteller at heart. He is a graduate of the Art Institute of Houston and lives in Texas with his family.

Kelly Parra is the author of YA novels *Graffiti Girl*, *Invisible Touch*, and other supernatural short stories. In addition to her independent works, Kelly works with Kevin Anderson & Associates on a variety of projects. She resides in Central Coast, California, with her husband and two children.

Andrea Rains Waggener is an author, novelist, ghostwriter, essayist, short story writer, screenwriter, copywriter, editor, poet, and a proud member of Kevin Anderson & Associates' team of writers. In a past she prefers not to remember much, she was a claims adjuster, JCPenney's catalog order-taker (before computers!), appellate court clerk, legal writing instructor, and lawyer. Writing in genres that vary from her chick-lit novel, *Alternate Beauty*, to her dog how-to book, *Dog Parenting*, to her self-help book, *Healthy, Wealthy, & Wise*, to ghostwritten memoirs to ghostwritten YA, horror, mystery, and mainstream fiction projects, Andrea still manages to find time to watch the rain and obsess over her dog and her knitting, art, and music projects. She lives with her husband and said dog on the Washington Coast, and if she isn't at home creating something, she can be found walking on the beach.

Inside the excruciatingly smelly and rough rodent costume, Lucia's left calf cramped up. The contracted muscle sent sharp shards of pain up and down her leg. She had to move.

Lucia shifted position, gently shaking her left leg to relieve the muscular stress. As she tried to work out the cramp, she turned to her right. Holding her breath, she scanned the backstage area around her. She exhaled in relief. She was alone. Or she hoped she was.

Mesmerized by the blood pool on the floor, Lucia hadn't paid attention to the Mimic's tapping footsteps when it had walked away wearing the bloody blue dog costume that contained Kelly's remains. Lucia had been in shock, she realized now. Her brain had stopped working. If it hadn't, she would have paid very close attention to those footfalls. Knowing where the Mimic went after it walked away was essential to Lucia's survival.

However, because she'd been devastated by the blow of losing Kelly, Lucia had dropped the mental ball. She had no idea where the Mimic was.

Even so, she had to move again. She needed to rest her legs. And she needed to think.

Lucia took another tentative step. Thankfully, the rodent-costume feet were fur covered. She made no sound as she moved around to the far side of the rubble pile that she and Kelly had been trying to move before the Mimic had appeared.

Lucia sank down onto a slanted concrete slab. She desperately wanted to take off the rodent head that covered her own sweating skull. But she couldn't be sure the Mimic wasn't hiding nearby. If it hadn't seen her yet, she was safer hidden inside the costume.

Lucia looked around the backstage area. The dim stage lights cast shadows over the darkened expanse, creating pockets of gloom amid the confusion of boxes, endoskeleton parts, and stage props. On Lucia's left, Nick's remains lay strewn across the floor in front of a half-open wardrobe. Out in front of Lucia, disturbingly, one of the stage lights spotlighted the blood pool that Kelly's death had left behind.

Even through the thick rodent mask, Lucia could smell the coppery odor of blood and the sickeningly sweet reek of decaying flesh and organs. Nick had been the first to die. His remains were already beginning to putrefy.

Although the adrenaline still coursing through Lucia's system was screaming at her to run, to get as far away from where she'd last seen the Mimic as she could, she knew that running would do her no good. Kelly's death was proof of that. There was nowhere in this tomb of a pizzeria where Lucia could safely hide. The deaths of the rest of the group had made that clear. No, for the moment, Lucia's best option was to stay where she was and get a handle on the situation.

Lucia stretched out her legs. Moving very slowly, she leaned over and massaged her constricted calf. The cramp was easing. Her muscles were relaxing.

Now that her brain was back online, Lucia realized there was only one way she was going to get out of this place alive. She had to kill the Mimic.

But how?

There must be a way, Lucia thought.

Although the Mimic seemed unbeatable, the logical part of Lucia's mind knew it wasn't. The Mimic wasn't some invincible supervillain. No, the creature, no matter what horrendous and homicidal things it did, was a machine. Machines could be destroyed.

But again—how?

Lucia closed her eyes and listened to the silence pressing around her. The silence should have been calming; it meant the Mimic wasn't approaching. But Lucia didn't feel calm. She felt tense and agitated. And under the distress, she felt desolate.

Lucia, not being the kind of mainstream kid who easily made friends, had spent much of her life in isolation. She wasn't the kind of girl to be invited to birthday parties. She never hung out after school with "the gang" or went shopping with the other girls in her class. This wasn't a bad thing. Lucia had little patience for what most girls liked talking about—endless chatting about clothes and boys. She preferred reading a book to shopping and pretty much everything else. She liked spending hours alone in her room, twirling in her hammock, immersed in learning something new or exploring a fictional world.

But being alone in an abandoned pizzeria, sharing the death-filled place with the torn and scattered remains of kids who, though not exactly friends, were familiar to Lucia, was nothing like hanging out alone in her room. This kind of alone felt like the ultimate isolation. Lucia was locked inside an abandoned building with a creature whose sole purpose was to find and kill her. No one knew she was here. She was alone. The only person who was going to help Lucia was Lucia.

An image of Kelly's face suddenly filled Lucia's mind. Just an hour before, or less (Lucia no longer had much grasp on passing time), Kelly had been joking with Lucia. Lucia had really liked Kelly. She'd thought she might have found someone who could be a good friend.

Poor Kelly, Lucia thought. She remembered how strained Kelly had looked before she'd put on the blue dog costume in the small costume room.

Lucia straightened.

Thinking of the costume room had triggered another memory. Lucia had a visceral recollection of touching the springlock mechanism inside the jester costume.

What if? Lucia thought.

Now that her mind had been stimulated, it whirred into action and went into overdrive. *What if*, Lucia asked herself again, *I could get the Mimic into that springlock costume?* If she could, maybe she could get the locks to activate and crush the creature.

But how would she get the locks to activate?

Lucia waved away the question. She'd worry about that point later. First, she had to figure out how to get the Mimic into the jester costume.

Lucia tried to ignore an itch at the back of her neck while she analyzed the problem from every angle. She squirmed; the rodent costume was getting scratchier by the second.

Rodents.

Lucia cocked her head. To trap a rodent, you created a situation where after it was where you wanted it to be, it had no choice but to go for the bait.

That's what Lucia had to do, she realized. Given that the Mimic would be looking for her, Lucia figured she'd put herself in the costume room and then make sure that the only costume the Mimic could get into was the jester costume.

Lucia looked around and listened. All was still and quiet.

She pushed herself up off the slab and stood. She cocked her head and listened again. No sound. No movement.

Well, she wasn't going to get far with her plan if she didn't move. Lucia sighed. She headed toward the costume room.

Lucia's plan was more easily thought up than executed. Once she'd returned to the costume room, she'd realized that disabling all the costumes except the jester costume was a daunting task.

Her first problem was that she felt compelled to stay in the rodent costume. In addition to its relentless gamey stink, it was abrading her skin to the point of fiery pain.

But Lucia didn't think it was wise to go costumeless. The Mimic could appear at any moment.

To have the dexterity needed for her costume-disabling task, therefore, the first thing Lucia had to do was tear away the ends of the rodent paw's fingertips. This she managed to do, nauseatingly, with her teeth. After that disgusting task, though, she still couldn't do what she needed to do. There were too many obstacles.

The yellow-walled, square costume room was crammed with eleven costumes besides the jester costume. The costumes hung from their heads on a stainless-steel rod that lined three of the room's walls. All eleven costumes had zipper access at both the front and the back. Lucia had to decommission twenty-two zippers.

Lucia stepped up to the costume at the end of the row—a green lizard. She tried to get a grip on the costume's front zipper. But she couldn't. The rodent costume head wasn't designed for up close work. If she stood upright and looked straight ahead, she could see through the rodent's mesh eyeholes. However, when she looked down, the costume head canted forward, and her vision was blocked.

Lucia tried shifting the head this way and that, but no matter what she did, the head kept getting in the way. Finally, feeling horribly exposed and vulnerable, Lucia removed the rodent head.

As soon as the head was off, Lucia took a long gulp of air. Although the air in the costume room was musty and dusty, it was a far cry better than the fetid odor inside the head.

Lucia pushed her matted, sweaty hair off her face and checked the doorway to be sure she was still alone. Soothed by the empty doorway, Lucia stepped over to the nearest costume and set her rodent head on the floor. She reached for the costume's front zipper. And that was when she discovered her next challenge.

In spite of freeing the fingertips of the rodent paws, Lucia didn't have the dexterity she needed to grasp the costume's zipper and manipulate it. The rodent paw fingers kept getting in the way, and she found herself fumbling instead of accomplishing much. Finally, Lucia relented and undid her costume's front zipper. Stepping out of the costume, she hissed when the room's cool air hit her abraded skin. Once again, she checked the doorway. She now felt even more horribly exposed. If the Mimic appeared, she was right out in the open—an easy target. And she still had another problem to solve.

After struggling with the lizard costume's front zipper for several minutes, Lucia discovered that zippers were not easily rendered inaccessible. When Lucia tried to break the zipper mechanism, she succeeded only in making the zipper awkward to manipulate but not unusable. Even when she broke off the top of the zipper, the rest of the zipper still functioned. If only she had a needle and thread, she'd be able to sew the costumes closed.

After she realized her task was harder than she'd originally expected it to be, Lucia thoroughly searched the room. A low-to-the-floor, scarred, warped pine shelf hugged one wall under some of the costumes. On that shelf, Lucia found a broken clipboard, a tangle of loose rope, an empty plastic water bottle, and several pens. She also found a metal rod that was leaning against the end of the shelf, perhaps a spare costume-hanging rod. She added the rod to the results of her little scavenger hunt.

You never knew what might come in handy. Unfortunately, she found no needles or thread.

Now what?

Lucia looked longingly at the empty water bottle. Her mouth was so parched it felt fuzzy. She wanted to go in search of water, but something told her she was running out of time.

Think! Lucia admonished herself.

Her gaze returned to the three pens she'd gathered. She felt a proverbial light bulb go off over her head. She grabbed the pens and rushed over to the lizard costume.

Jamming the pen into the zipper, just below the top of it, Lucia gouged at the zipper's little metal teeth until two of them bent. She tried to pull down the zipper. It wouldn't get past the bent teeth.

"Yes!"

Lucia cringed at how loud her voice sounded in the little room. She quickly looked around to be sure she was still alone. She was. It was just her and the jester and the other eleven costumes, hanging motionless near the room's walls.

Now that she knew what to do, Lucia worked quickly. She disabled the lizard's second zipper, and then she began stabbing at the top of every zipper she found. Bending the zipper teeth wasn't easy—it was an awkward and slow task. But she was making progress. She'd reached the sixth costume and was on its second zipper. But that was as far as she got before her situation became far more desperate than she'd already known it was.

All the costumes began to sway.

Lucia froze.

She hadn't touched the other costumes. And they wouldn't have started moving on their own.

Lucia's heart rate doubled as she stared at the undulating costumes. She took a step back away from them.

When the Mimic had extricated itself from the mushroom costume to kill Kelly, Lucia had learned that she couldn't rely on flickering lights to warn her of the Mimic's presence. For some reason, the Mimic's effect on the lights wasn't a consistent byproduct of the Mimic's location.

Even without the flickering lights, though, the Mimic's approach in a room as small as this one wasn't something Lucia would have missed. The costume room's door was open, yes, but it had been within her line of sight the entire time she'd been in here. That meant . . .

The Mimic had already been in the room when Lucia had started trying to disable the costumes.

Goose bumps instantly covered Lucia's skin. A shiver rippled through her body.

For a half second, Lucia considered running. She immediately dismissed the idea. How could she complete her plan if she did that?

Lucia quickly scanned the swinging costumes. Which one was the Mimic in?

Not the first six, obviously. Lucia's throat constricted with the realization of how lucky she'd been. What if the Mimic had been inside one of the costumes she'd fiddled with?

Well, that question was easy to answer. She'd be dead.

Lucia quickly grabbed the rodent costume and pulled it on. Zipping it up fast, she stuffed her head into the tumes that still had working zippers. They didn't move.

So, Lucia, once again disguised as a tattered rodent, slipped behind the already-tampered-with costumes.

What should she do now?

Well, she couldn't just hide among the costumes forever. The Mimic would crawl out and kill her if she did.

She had to stick with her task. When the Mimic did reveal itself, chances were that it would attempt to enter another costume. She wanted to be sure the only costume available to it was the springlock jester.

Inching to her left, Lucia moved as stealthily as possible to the next costume. She managed to grasp the zipper pull and ease down its back zipper. Then she did her best to peer into it through the rodent's mesh eyeholes. Thankfully, she was able to see well enough to tell that the costume was empty. She let out a quiet breath of relief. Fumbling with the pen through the rodent paw fur, she jabbed at the costume's zipper with her pen. It took three tries to bend the zipper teeth because her hand wouldn't stop shaking.

Finally, she finished with the seventh costume. She moved on.

Her blood rushing so loudly through her veins that it sounded like a swarm of bees in her ears, Lucia managed to get through two more costumes. When she faced the tenth costume, she barely had the will to raise her hands to its zipper. At this point, she was playing a very dangerous game of Russian roulette, and she was down to even odds of losing.

It was't a surprise, therefore, when her luck ran out

Nerve-wracking micrometer by micrometer, Lucia began lowering the zipper on the tenth costume, a dark brown gopher. Lucia paused and looked into the costume, past the top of the zipper. The gopher costume didn't move, but the pale glow of the room's dim overhead bulb glinted weakly off something metal.

Lucia's hand turned to stone. She stopped breathing.

The Mimic was inside the gopher.

Lucia immediately withdrew her trembling hand. She started retreating from the gopher.

Once again, Lucia's adrenaline system commanded her to run. She ignored the imperative. She slid her feet back inch by inch until she was half a foot from the gopher. Then she began to sidestep away from it.

That's when the gopher moved. Its shoulder fluttered like a small tic. And then the gopher's arm came up.

Lucia's adrenaline overrode her intellect. She ran.

She wasn't able to run far, though. When the gopher's arm raised, its zipper immediately lowered, and the Mimic, in all its spine-chilling spidery awfulness, lurched up and out the back of the gopher. The Mimic leaped away from the gopher, its groping limbs extending and expanding, searching and probing. It began writhing through the arms and legs of the rest of the costumes.

Lucia had only made it to the end of the row of costumes when the Mimic began to slink around the room. She had to duck between a blackbird costume and a purple lion costume to avoid one of the Mimic's inquisitive metal appendages.

Now that the Mimic was here, creeping around mere inches from Lucia, she began to doubt the wisdom of her plan. If the Mimic found her, what did it matter if the costumes were disabled? She'd never have a chance to lure the Mimic to the springlock jester.

The room was too small. And it was too cramped. Hidden among the costumes, Lucia couldn't see well enough to stay away from the Mimic. No matter what she did, the danger of it catching her unawares was ever present.

What if she ran from the costume room? Could she get far enough ahead of the Mimic to outrun it?

No. The way the Mimic moved in its current configuration made it clear that it could move faster and more nimbly than something on two legs, especially a scared something encumbered by a rodent costume. Lucia would have no chance if she ran.

Lucia huddled between the blackbird and the lion, hunched forward in an attempt to make herself the smallest, most inconspicuous rodent possible. Nearby—too nearby—the Mimic scrabbled among the costumes.

Lucia's gaze darted left and right as she tried to keep up with the Mimic's movements. She didn't dare turn her head to help her track the thing. Her only hope at this point was to stay hidden long enough for it to either lose interest or climb into another suit. Thanks to her efforts, only two suits were usable: the last one that Lucia hadn't had time to disable—a flat-furred, holey tiger costume—and the springlock jester. Lucia had a fifty-fifty chance that the Mimic would get into the right costume.

But not if it got to her first. Which it did.

Lucia gasped when she suddenly found herself staring into the Mimic's white glowing eyes. It was right in front of her! The Mimic was looking through the mesh of the rodent's eyes, gazing right into Lucia's own eyes.

Lucia couldn't turn and run fast enough, but she had another choice. She didn't hesitate. She quickly reached behind her and fumbled for the zipper at the rodent's back.

Lucia started tugging on the metal pull at the top of the zipper. Her frantic fingers slipped off it, but she immediately grabbed it again.

Panting in panic, Lucia yanked the zipper pull downward. As she did, she felt something sharp graze her lip. She flinched and reared her head back inside the costume head.

The Mimic was starting to crawl into the rodent costume through the rodent's mouth!

The Mimic's cold metal pressed against Lucia's chin. The feel of the unrelenting pressure made Lucia's skin crawl. She redoubled her efforts to get the zipper down.

"Come on! Come on!" she chanted. There was no point in being silent now.

Lucia's head began to compress against the back of the rodent costume head; the Mimic was pushing in farther and farther. Lucia tried to tuck her head away from the Mimic as far as she could.

And finally, the zipper was down.

Lucia quickly ducked down and shot backward out of the rodent. The costume fell away from her, folding itself over the encroaching Mimic. The Mimic was immediately engulfed in scrappy gray fur, and it flailed its metallic limbs to get control of the rodent costume.

Lucia took advantage of the nanosecond of opportunity. Thankfully, in spite of her terror, Lucia's brain was still functioning. Either that or her fear was bypassing her brain and driving her actions. Whatever was motivating her, Lucia immediately scampered through the costumes and dove for the pile of things she'd found earlier during her exploration of the room. Grabbing the rope, she rushed back to the rodent costume, which was still writhing as the Mimic fought to get control of it.

Sweat cascading down between her shoulder blades, her tangled curls nearly blinding her, Lucia bent down in front of the rodent costume legs. Quickly, she looped the rope around the ankles of the costume and cinched it up tight.

"Please work," she whispered as she raised up again and backed away from the rodent Mimic.

Lucia retreated a few feet more. She watched the rodent's fur bunch up and bulge out as the Mimic moved inside it.

When the rodent began to step forward, Lucia turned and ran across the small room. She took cover behind the jester costume. There, she peered around the raspberry-pink side of the jester's tunic and watched the rodent.

The Mimic, inside the rodent suit, started toward the jester.

It immediately toppled forward.

It worked! Lucia cheered silently.

With the rodent's legs tied together, the Mimic couldn't walk.

But it could still move.

Lucia's triumph was short-lived.

She suppressed a sigh as she watched a metallic limb jut out through the rodent costume's mouth. Inevitably, that limb was followed by another and then another. The Mimic, like a segmented worm, began edging itself out of the rodent, one metal section at a time.

As each section escaped the gray fur, Lucia heard a menacing click.

Click, click, click. The Mimic extracted itself from the suit like an expanding viper. Although it was made of metal, it looked like a pulsing, squirming snake. It slithered free of the rodent costume and then, with another set of clicks combined with a bone-rattling clacking, it reconfigured itself into its upright form.

The bare bulb overhead flickered.

Now what do I do? Lucia asked herself.

For the moment, she was out of the Mimic's line of sight. She was tucked behind the jester, and she was as still as she knew how to be. But she didn't think she'd be hidden for long, not when the Mimic started to move around.

But the Mimic didn't move. It just stood in the middle of the room. Its head turned to the left. Then it turned to the right. Its joints whirred.

Lucia felt nausea rise up her throat. She grimaced and swallowed it back down.

She couldn't outlast the Mimic in a "wait and see what comes next" scenario. She needed to take action. Running wasn't the right thing to do. She knew that. How could she outsmart the thing?

The Mimic suddenly turned. Lucia quivered, and she brushed against the silky material of the jester costume.

Even as she blenched at the movement, she got an idea. And she'd have to be fast.

Not worrying about the sounds she made or how much the jester costume moved, Lucia reached out and felt for the seam at the back of the jester's neck. Slipping her fingers along the seam, she found a gap and pried the stitching open.

Thankfully, although the costume was in better shape than the others in the room, it was still old. The joint line at the back of the neck gave way easily. In seconds, Lucia was able to pull it apart far enough to shove her head through the opening.

Although sticking her head inside a springlock suit wasn't Lucia's idea of a supergood plan, it was all she could think of. And it was just her head. She had no intention of fully getting into the suit.

All she needed to do was get the Mimic's attention. If it thought she was in the suit, it would come for her.

And that was what Lucia was counting on. She wanted the Mimic to try to do to her what it had done to Kelly.

The Mimic continued to look around the room, but it didn't look toward the jester. Lucia wasn't about to move while her head was inside a springlock suit. So, she held perfectly still and called out, "Come and get me!"

The Mimic's head spun toward the jester. In the blink of an eye, it lunged.

Lucia knew the timing had to be perfect. And she got lucky.

Just as the Mimic surged toward the front of the jester suit, shoving itself through the opening in the jester's chest, Lucia jerked her head back out of the jester head. The Mimic, already committed to its incursion into the jester costume, didn't notice Lucia's exit. It continued to conform itself into the jester's body shape, tucking all its metal parts inside the half-pink, half-greenish costume.

Lucia again didn't have a lot of time. It wouldn't take long for the Mimic to realize she wasn't in the suit.

As Lucia listened to the last of the Mimic's endoskeleton ratchet into place inside the jester costume, she spun and darted toward the metal rod she'd found earlier.

up Lucia's arms as she whacked the suit again and again and again.

Each whack resounded through the room with a muffled clank. Lucia resumed her earlier chant. "Come on! Come on! Come on!"

According to what Lucia had read, the springlocks were far too easily triggered. The blows she was landing on the suit should get the locks to engage.

But the springlocks didn't activate.

Instead, the Mimic began climbing back out of the jester's mouth.

Lucia tamped down her dismay and continued to clobber the suit. Still, the springlocks didn't trigger.

The compressed pleating of metal that the Mimic had managed to free from the jester's mouth began to dilate. It enlarged itself and morphed itself into the Mimic's head. The Mimic's gaze latched onto Lucia. It opened its mouth.

In an instant, Lucia switched strategies. She immediately repositioned her grip on the metal rod, and she hefted it like a spear, stabbing the end of the rod as deeply into the Mimic's mouth as she possibly could get it.

The Mimic's head was jolted savagely back. And finally, the springlocks were set off. The room was immediately filled with the clamoring cascade of metal striking metal. The jester suit convulsed.

Shaking as if caught in the vortex of a hurricane, the suit gyrated, surging right and left, up and down. Every square inch of the jester moved at once. It quaked and rattled so fast that watching it was dizzying.

But Lucia didn't look away. She couldn't. Her gaze was held in both fascination and revulsion. And it was held in hope. Would the springlocks do what she needed them to do?

Lucia let out a whoop when she got the answer to her question.

Viscous black fluid began seeping through the jester's bright fabric. Pooling at the costume's joints, the fluid gave off the powerful smell of engine oil. The pungent eye-watering odor clogged Lucia's nostrils, but a flower couldn't have smelled sweeter in that moment.

Lucia couldn't afford to linger any longer, though. She could see that the springlocks were impaling the Mimic, but would they do enough damage to disable it? Lucia couldn't count on that.

Gripping the metal rod, Lucia turned and ran out of the costume room. As soon as she was through the door, she slammed it shut behind her.

Because it was a hidden door, it had interlocking inset handles that worked in conjunction with a latch on the wall. Lucia was able to shove the metal rod through the opening in the door handles and the wall latch, effectively bracing the door closed.

Lucia's flight-or-fight response fired up. Her legs twitched in their need to force her into a run. But Lucia stood fast.

As she'd already concluded, running and hiding wasn't a long-term solution to her problem. She needed to find a way out of the building. And to do that, she had to have time. She couldn't concentrate on getting out if she was constantly in fear of the Mimic's return.

No. It had to end here. Or not. Either way, she needed to know.

Lucia stood her ground and stared at the door. Rubbing her arms to settle herself, she concentrated on slowing her galloping heart rate.

Even though she was trying to contain her fear, Lucia remained poised. She balanced on the balls of her feet. Every muscle in her body was contracted into a prepare-to-run position.

She kept her gaze on the door. And on the metal rod. She was alert to even the tiniest tremor on the flat wood or round metal surfaces.

But both remained motionless.

Lucia counted to sixty. Then she did it again. And one more time.

Finally, Lucia scrounged up some courage. She sank to her knees and crept forward until she could bend over and see through the crack under the door.

Closing one eye, Lucia peered into the small costume room. A gasp caught at the back of her throat when she saw the jester costume writhing on the floor in a widening sticky black stain of thick liquid.

The Mimic was still moving, but its movements were chaotic and frantic. It was no longer the menace in control. It was the victim.

Lucia realized that now was her chance. The Mimic was vulnerable. She had to act. If she waited, the Mimic might find a way to self-repair.

Lucia got off the floor. She stood and set her shoulders.

Taking a deep breath, she reached out and pulled the rod away from the door handles. She opened the door.

Half expecting the Mimic to suddenly erupt from the floor and charge at her, Lucia forced herself to step into the room. Breathing shallowly so the black oil fumes didn't make her sick, Lucia walked toward the Mimic.

The Mimic might have seen Lucia; its head still protruded from the jester's mouth, and its eyes were still glowing. The glow, however, was fading . . . or least Lucia thought it was.

Lucia hesitated, but the Mimic made no attempt to come at her. It just continued to flop around in the black goo.

Lucia summoned up all the nerve she had. She dashed forward and stepped into the spreading oil. Positioning herself behind the Mimic, Lucia swiftly crouched down and reached out a hand. Calling up her memory of what she'd read about the Mimic in the user's manual, she felt around the back of its head. She nearly cried in joy when her fingers located what she was looking for. She gripped the small switch she'd found. She flipped it.

The Mimic went slack. The jester costume stilled.

The creature was deactivated. It was over.

A ray of sunshine blinded Lucia as she braced her torn and bleeding hands against the hot, coarse exterior wall of the abandoned pizzeria that she'd thought was going to be her final resting place. Balancing on her tiptoes, she pushed off the table she'd dragged into place to access the tiny window set high on the wall at the far end of the ladies' restroom.

Once Lucia had the building to herself, after she was sure that she was no longer being hunted, she'd been able to calmly (sort of... she was still jumpy) assess every potential exit in the building. All the doors and windows were barricaded with concrete and wood or metal, but the small window in the ladies' restroom had less concrete and metal than the others.

Even so, it had taken what had felt like hours of prodding and shoving at concrete blocks, prying at the metal that had been riveted to the wall over the window, and pounding at heavy boards nailed into place over the glass, before she could bash the glass and scrape it away from the window frame. Then she had to do some painful squirming through the small opening to create the egress she needed. But now she was on her way out.

"Hey!" a deep male voice called out. "What are you doing?"

It was a nice voice. A young voice. A kind voice. Was it real or was she imagining it?

Lucia shielded her eyes with the back of her hand. She squinted toward the sound of the voice. She tried to push herself farther out the window but she couldn't. She was spent. Beyond exhausted. She had nothing else left.

Suddenly, strong, calloused hands were gripping her forearms.

"What happened to you?" the same voice asked.

Something blocked the sun, and Lucia looked into a pair of gentle blue eyes under a bright orange hard hat. A construction worker! She wasn't imagining her rescuer.

She felt herself being dragged through the window opening.

Lucia felt tears start to spill down her face. The salty liquid stung the abrasions on her cheeks.

"Hey, it's okay," the construction worker said. "I've got you."

Lucia tried to speak but her mouth was too dry. She was, however, able to smile.